Join the Ghostwriter T[...]
You How [...]

- Put together a detective kit for supersleuths
- Create lots of secret codes
- Discover how to write invisible messages
- Use disguises to track down criminals
- Find, lift, and identify fingerprints
- And more!

Read the Solve-It-Yourself Mysteries . . .

Follow the Ghostwriter team and see if *you* can solve:

- The Marathon Mystery Message
- The Case of the Shocking-Pink Envelope
- The Case of the One-Armed Shoplifter

and

Find the Hidden Secret Messages from Ghostwriter That Only *You* Can Decipher . . .

- Then use the special decoder wheel you'll find right in this book to answer Ghostwriter's final question on page 75!

Join the Team!

Do you watch GHOSTWRITER on PBS? Then you know that when you read and write to solve a mystery or unravel a puzzle, you're using the same smarts and skills the Ghostwriter team uses.

We hope you'll join the team and read along to help solve the mysterious and puzzling goings-on in these GHOSTWRITER books!

THE Ghost writer™

DETECTIVE GUIDE

TOOLS AND TRICKS OF THE TRADE

by

Susan Lurie

Illustrated by Felipe Galindo

A CHILDREN'S TELEVISION WORKSHOP BOOK

BANTAM BOOKS
NEW YORK · TORONTO · LONDON · SYDNEY · AUCKLAND

THE GHOSTWRITER DETECTIVE GUIDE

A Bantam Book / November 1992

Ghostwriter **Ghost**writer and ●
are trademarks of Children's Television Workshop.
All rights reserved. Used under authorization.

Art direction by Marva Martin
Cover photo by Walt Chrynwski
Cover design by Susan Herr
Interior illustrations by Felipe Galindo

ISBN 0-553-48069-3

Published simultaneously in the United States and Canada

Bantam Books are published by Bantam Books, a division of Bantam
Doubleday Dell Publishing Group, Inc. Its trademark, consisting of the
words "Bantam Books" and the portrayal of a rooster, is Registered in
U.S. Patent and Trademark Office and in other countries. Marca Registrada. Bantam Books, 1540 Broadway, New York, New York 10036.

THE GHOSTWRITER TEAM MEMBERS STARRING IN THIS BOOK ARE...

Jamal Jenkins

Lenni Frazier

Ghostwriter

Alex Fernandez

Gaby Fernandez

GADGET DETECTIVE KIT

Here's everything you need for your on-the-go investigations. From pens to notebooks to fingerprint powder and clue-catching tweezers, our kit doesn't leave out a thing!

Check off each item as you put your detective kit together. Then check out the name that's hidden on these pages. Just circle the boldface letters you find in each item on the checklist. Write those letters, in the order they appear, in the blank spaces at the top of the page.

We circled the first one to get you started.

Detective Kit Checklist

____ Magnifying **g**lass for making small clues appear bigger

_____ Flashlight
for looking under counters and in dark corners

_____ Notebook and pen
for writing down clues and facts

_____ Envelopes and bags
for collecting clues

_____ Tape measure
for measuring distances

_____ Tweezers
for picking up small clues, such as hairs and threads

_____ Artist's small paintbrush
for brushing on fingerprint powder

——	Lead pencil and sandpaper	for making dark fingerprint powder
——	Talcum powder	for making light fingerprint powder
——	Roll of clear tape	for taping over fingerprints
——	Scissors	for cutting the tape you use to pick up fingerprints

You'll find out more about fingerprints on page 52.

JAMAL'S SECRET CODE JOKES

Knowing secret codes can be important when you're solving a case. On the Ghostwriter team we often have to decode secret messages. Also, I like to send coded messages to Alex. He's a real code nut. Here's one of my favorites, the Tic-Tac-Toe code! Use it to find the answers to the jokes on the next page.

Here's how to make it:

1. Draw three tic-tac-toe boards. Leave one blank. Put dots in the other two boards, as you see in the picture.

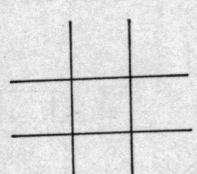 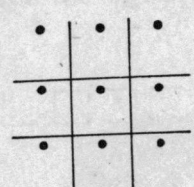 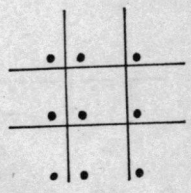

2. Write the letters of the alphabet like this:

A	B	C
D	E	F
G	H	I

J	K	L
M	N	O
P	Q	R

S	T	U
V	W	X
Y	Z	

3. The patterns of lines or lines and dots now stand for the letters in the alphabet. Here's how my name looks in the Tic-Tac-Toe code:

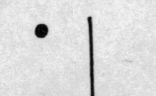 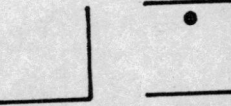  

Write your name in Tic-Tac-Toe code here:

_____

Now figure out the answers to my Tic-Tac-Totally secret jokes!

1. What did the garbage collector say to the thief?

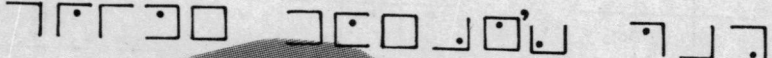

2. Why didn't the bald detective have any keys?

Because he didn't have any

3. What's the difference between a jeweler and a jailer?

A jeweler

A jailer

GABY'S GHOSTWRITER
DECODER WHEEL

There's no getting around it! You'll need a decoder wheel to decipher the message that Ghostwriter left you on the next page. So here's how to put your decoder wheel together—and how to use it!

What You Need:

- Scissors
- Alphabet and Code wheels on page 85
- Thumbtack or paper fastener

What to Do:

1. Cut out the big Alphabet Wheel and the small Code Wheel on page 85.
2. Put the Code Wheel on top of the Alphabet Wheel, as you see in the picture.

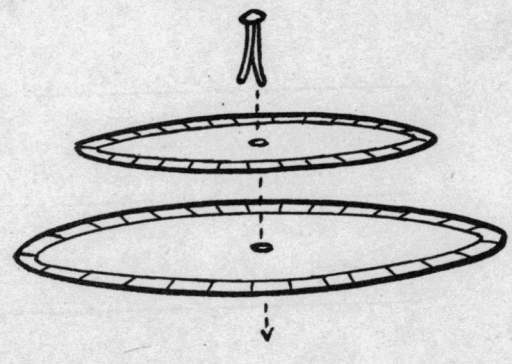

3. Push the thumbtack or paper fastener through the center dots of the wheels. Bend the tabs of the fastener to hold the wheels in place.

How to Use Your Decoder Wheel:

1. Ghostwriter's message below is written in Code G. This means that A = G. Turn the small wheel so that the letter G is under the letter A on the big wheel.
2. Find each letter in Ghostwriter's message on the small wheel. Write down the letter it lines up with on the big wheel.

Message: Znkxk'y g ykixkz skyygmk ot znoy huuq.
Nuc corr eua lotj oz? Cnkxk ynuarj eua
ruuq? Xkgj zu znk ktj. Zngz'y se irak.
Znkt eua'rr qtuc payz cngz zu ju.

Translation: _____

_____

_____

_____

3. To write a message in code, find each letter of your message on the big wheel. Write down the letter it lines up with on the small wheel.

Write a secret message to a friend using Code F!

MY STERIO USSEC RETMES SAGES

Do you know what the above title says? You will, once I show you my favorite secret codes.

1. Split It

This is one of my best codes. It's easy to do, and it always stumps people who don't know how to crack it. Just write down a sentence. Then split the letters so that each word looks completely different.

If you split . . .
Where was the detective when the lights went out?
. . . it would look like this:
Whe rew as thede tect ivew hent heligh tswen tout?

Now read the answer to my next joke using the **Split It** code.

Answer

2. Switch It

This is also a great code. Just switch the last letter of each word with the first letter of the next word.

If you switch...

Where was the detective when the lights went out?

...it would look like this:

Wherw eat shd eetectivw ehet nhl eightw seno tut?

Now read the answer to my sister Gaby's joke using the **Switch It** code.

Answer

3. Spin It

This is my old standby code. All you have to do is spell each sentence backward.

If you spin . . .

Where was the detective when the lights went out?

. . . it would look like this:

Tuo tnew sthgil eht nehw evitceted eht saw erehw?

Use the **Spin It** code to read the answer.

Krad eht ni.

_____

Answer

4. Split It? Switch It? Spin It?

Now figure out which code to use to read: **My sterio ussec retmes sages!**

LENNI'S LINES

I'm here to show you my lineup of secret codes. All you need to make them are some long, thin strips of paper, a pencil, a pen, and a piece of string.

1. Strip It

Mark 26 spaces on a strip of paper. Then write the letters of the alphabet, one letter in each space. This is your Alphabet Strip. On another strip of paper, mark 52 spaces and write the alphabet twice. This is your Code Strip.

Alphabet Strip ◄

A	B	C	D	E	F	G	H	I	J	K	L	M	N	O	P	Q	R	S	T	U	V	W	X	Y	Z

Now you're ready to use the **Strip It** decoder.
Write your best friend's name here:

_____

Now write his or her name in Code X.

_____

Code Strip ◆

Here's how: Slide the *A* in the Alphabet Strip over the first *X* in the Code Strip. Find each letter of your friend's name on the Alphabet Strip. Write down the letter it lines up with on the Code Strip. That's all there is to it!

2. **Wrap It**

Take a strip of paper. Tape one end of the strip to one end of a pencil. Wrap the strip around the pencil tightly and tape the other end. Write your secret message on the strip of paper. Unroll the paper. Your message will be scrambled. When your friends rewrap the paper strip around their pencils, your message will reappear. Try it!

3. **String It**

Trace the letters on the alphabet strip on the next page. Hold a piece of string along the strip, as you see in the picture. Make a dot with a pen at the tip of the string. Next make a dot at the first letter of your message. For example, if your first word is *secret*, make a dot at the S. Move this dot to Start, and make another dot above the *E*. Now move this dot to Start before you make the next dot above the C.

Trace the alphabet strip below again and give it to a friend. Then you can write secret messages to each other in my **String It** code!

A B C D E F G H I J K L M N O P Q R S T U V W X Y Z

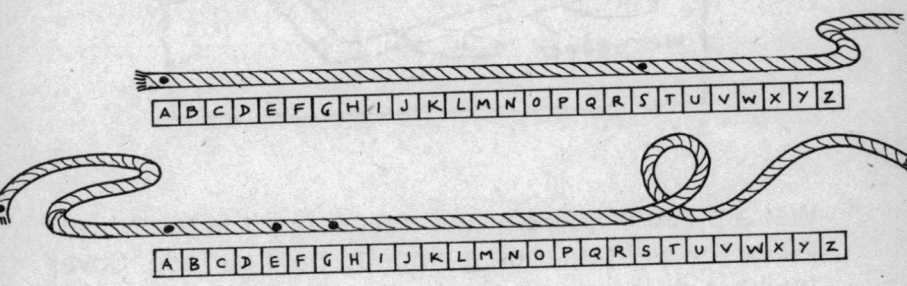

TH*IN*K AGAIN

What do you do when you really want to keep a secret message a secret? Make it invisible! Write it on the back of a letter. Or write it in the blank spaces between the lines. Otherwise, someone might get suspicious when he or she sees you reading a blank piece of paper!

Here are two different ways to make your messages invisible.

1. Write with Water

Wet a piece of paper—and make sure it is really wet! Place the wet paper on a smooth, hard surface. Cover it with a dry piece of paper and write firmly on the dry paper with a toothpick. If you hold the wet paper up to the light, you will see your message on it. It will disappear when the paper dries and reappear when it's wet again.

2. Use a Candle

Wax a piece of paper by rubbing it with a white candle. Place the waxed side down on a blank piece of paper. Using a toothpick, write your message firmly so that the wax is transferred to the blank paper.

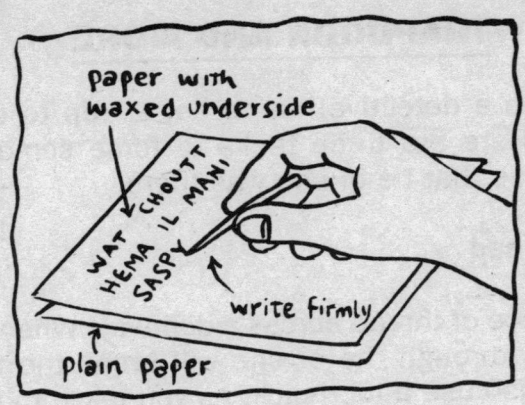

To read your message, sprinkle the paper with black pepper. Shake the paper gently. Pepper powder will stick to the wax and you'll see your message.

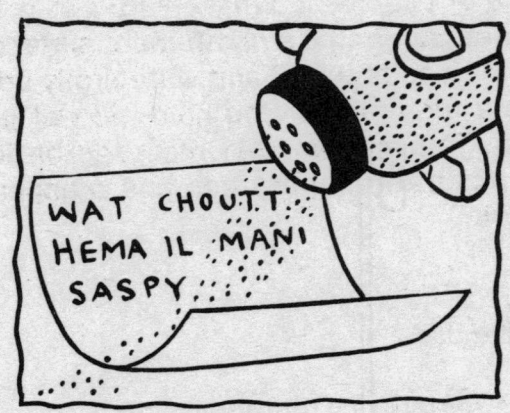

Split It! Switch It! Spin It! Use one of Alex's secret codes to read the message above.

TRAPDOOR AND MORE

Sometimes a detective has to set a trap to catch a suspect. Here are three tricks to force someone to leave a clue that he or she was there.

A little thread . . .

Tape a piece of thread across a doorway. When someone walks through, he or she will break the thread. You can also use a toothpick: As you leave the room, close the door on the toothpick. If someone opens the door while you are out, you will find the toothpick on the floor when you return.

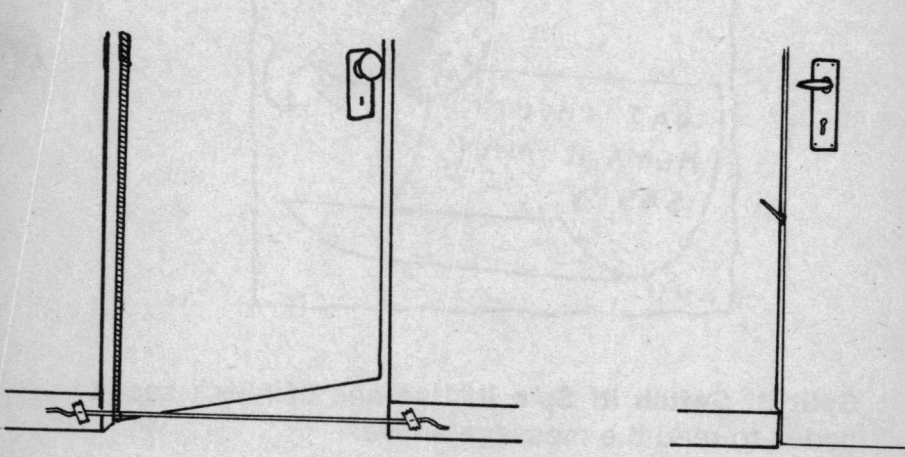

A piece of hair...

Glue a strand of hair across the opening crack of a drawer or door. If the door or drawer is opened, the hair will come unglued.

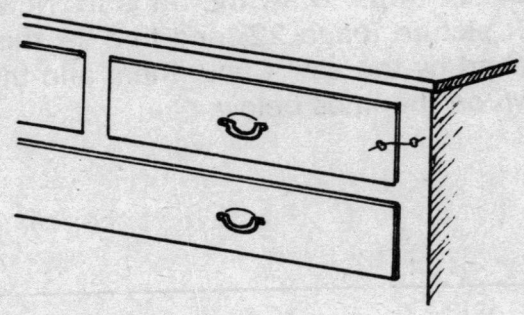

A tiny mark...

Draw a tiny line that runs across two pieces of paper. Chances are, if the papers are moved, the line will be broken.

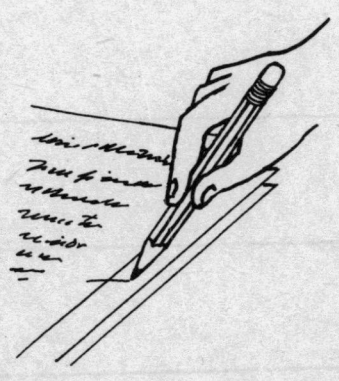

JAMAL'S ROOM—BEFORE AND AFTER!

Oh, no! Someone's been snooping in my room. Look at the BEFORE picture and find three places where I could have set traps. Draw the traps in. Now look at the AFTER picture (page 22) and find six things that were touched by the spy! Circle them and then write them down on the lines below.

1. _____

2. _____

3. _____

4. _____

5. _____

6. _____

BEFORE

AFTER

GABY'S SHADOW POWER

What do you do when you're spotted shadowing a suspect? It's time for a quick change! What do I mean? You'll see—just keep reading. Shadow power is all about changing the way you look!

Start out with these quick disguises.

1. **Become a one-armed detective...**

Put your arm in a sling. Or take one arm out of the sleeve of your coat. Tuck the empty sleeve into your coat pocket. If you're spotted, take off the sling! Put your arm back into your sleeve!

2. **Change your walk...**

There are all kinds of walking styles. Some people walk with tiny steps. Other people glide. And still other people take big, bouncy steps. One great way to disguise yourself is to change the way you walk. You'll be surprised at how much it changes the way you look! And get this: You don't need any props, like slings. All you need is your eyes—and your imagination!

Go outside and watch people as they walk by. Take notes on what you see. Then try to imitate some of the walks you saw. If you're imitating a person who takes small steps, imagine you have a rope around your knees that stops you from stepping out. If you're imitating a person with a bouncy walk, imagine you have balloons tied to your shoulders pulling you up.

Use your disguises along with big hats, colorful scarves, and sunglasses! Put them on and take them off for *Shadow Power!*

THE MARATHON MYSTERY MESSAGE

It was a beautiful sunny day in November and everyone was excited about the Big Bike Marathon. Millions . . . no, maybe thousands . . . well, hundreds of bikers were racing. There were exactly 192 more than last year! Best of all, the halfway point was right on my street! You know I was watching—along with Tina, Alex, Lenni, and Jamal. We thought we'd just be there to cheer the bikers on. And I thought I might find a new story for GabNews, my newspaper. There are hundreds . . . no, thousands . . . maybe millions of stories in Brooklyn just waiting to be told. And maybe I'd even be on the news. All of the local TV stations would be there covering the race. You see, you never know what's going to happen. We sure didn't know we'd be the ones to save the race!

—from Gaby's journal

"Here they come!" Alex said, looking far down the street. "I heard some of the racers were fighting on TV this morning."

"Everybody knows how Ace Chasen hates last year's winner, Winnie Slocum," Tina said as she fiddled with her video camera.

"Winnie 'Win'!" Gaby cheered. "She's so cool."

"Ace said Win cheated her out of first place last year by giving her a flat tire," Tina said. "Do you think it's true?"

"Win Slocum would never cheat!" Gaby protested.

"Well, Ace says that Win Slocum won't even finish the race this year," Alex said.

"Well, then, it looks like she's wrong," Jamal said. He pointed. "That's Win Slocum in the lead!"

The bikes were whizzing toward Gaby and her friends. Everyone recognized Winnie Slocum's bright yellow unitard. Lenni started cheering, and soon people in the crowd joined in. Gaby heard cheers in at least six different languages.

Pedaling behind Winnie was Ace Chasen, who was dressed in black. She looked tired. Behind them both was a girl on a silver racing bike. She wore a pink unitard, and her face was bright red under her black helmet. "I don't think she'll be in this race much longer," Gaby told everyone. "A red face is a sure sign of exhaustion."

Right then a person in a baggy trench coat and a rain hat stepped out of the crowd. "That's weird," Lenni said to Gaby. "It's a warm day. No need for a coat and a hat."

The oddly dressed person reached into a pocket, pulled something out, lit it, and tossed it into the street. Flashes and bangs filled the race course.

"Firecrackers!" Alex cried. "Look out!"

The firecrackers were going off right in front of Winnie Slocum's bike. She tried to swerve and another biker crashed into her. They went down together, and more racers piled into them.

Jamal winced. "Ow! What a mess."

"I'm going to help," Alex said. He ran toward the piled-up bikers. Jamal and Lenni went with him.

"Winnie's down!" Gaby cried. "I think she's hurt."

"Uh-huh," Tina said, her eye glued to the viewfinder of her video camera. "This'll be great!" She zoomed in on the big crash scene. "Maybe one of the local news stations will show this tape!"

"I doubt it," Gaby said, standing on tiptoes to peer across the crowd. "I see camera crews from all of the stations right here."

Since Gaby was shorter than most of the people around her, she couldn't see much of what was being done to help the crashed bikers. But she did see something strange across the street. The third-place racer, the one on the silver bike, was pulling out of a dark alleyway. She looked a lot better than she had a few minutes ago.

The crowd broke up as people helped the hurt bikers move to the sidelines. Winnie Slocum limped over to a lamppost and leaned her bike against it. Those who weren't hurt climbed back onto their bikes and continued the race. This time Ace Chasen was in the lead.

Lenni and Jamal came back. The police had asked Alex to be a witness. He was still at the crash site talking to a police officer.

"This race is turning out to be more exciting than I expected!" Lenni said. Jamal was quickly scribbling a description of the scene on his notepad.

"What are the rules of the race?" Gaby asked Jamal. "Is it okay for someone to leave the route? You know, not go very far but sort of go off course?"

"What are you talking about?" he said.

"I saw one of the racers come out of that alley across the street. Why would someone go down there when everyone is going that way?" Gaby pointed down the street.

"Maybe you saw it wrong," Lenni suggested. She led the way down the street.

As they passed Lee DeNoto's Bowling Alley, Gaby saw that the words on the sign had been changed to:

GO IN ALLEY   SEE NOTE

"That's a message from Ghostwriter," Gaby whispered to Jamal.

"Well, we'd better go check it out," he said.

They crossed the street, just in time to see a person in a trench coat and a floppy rain hat come running out of the alley.

"Hey," Lenni said. "Wasn't that the person who threw—?"

Before she could finish the sentence, the figure disappeared into the crowd.

The team headed into the alley. There wasn't anything there. No flat bike tires. No empty water bottles. Not one sign of a biker stopping to fix anything.

Lenni was already turning to leave when Gaby spotted a crumpled piece of paper on the ground. She picked the paper up and spread it out. It was a note!

But what did it say? The message made no sense.

HIT WIN! HEREWES WITCH TOW IN THER ACE.

"I don't get it," Gaby said.

Lenni read over her shoulder. "It must be a secret message."

Jamal got out his notepad and wrote the message down. He read it three times but still couldn't come up with anything. Then he wrote "Ghostwriter, please show us only the real words."

Ghostwriter went to work. The words on the pad swirled into two lines, like this:

HIT WIN WITCH TOW IN ACE
HEREWES THER

Jamal showed the pad to Lenni.

"'Hit win witch tow in ace'? That still doesn't make any sense," Lenni complained.

"Try writing it backward," Jamal wrote, and the words appeared like this:

ECA REHT NI WOT HCTIW SEWEREH !NIW TIH.

"That didn't work either," Jamal muttered.

"Too bad Alex isn't here. He's the king of codes," Gaby said.

"Mix them up," Jamal wrote to Ghostwriter.

But no matter how the words were placed, they didn't make a real message.

"Well, it must be from somebody named Ace," Lenni said. "Ace Chasen, maybe?" Her eyes widened. "And it says to 'Hit Win.' That could mean Winnie Slocum!"

Tina gasped. "And now Winnie is out of the race," she said. "I have film of her crashing. If Ace can stay at the front of the pack, she'll probably win."

"That won't be easy," Jamal said. "There's still a long way to go. The finish line is in Central Park."

"Whew!" Gaby exclaimed. "If I pedaled that long, my legs would fall off. It's five and a half miles from here to Central Park."

"How do you know that?" Jamal asked. Then he waved his hand. "Forget I asked. Anyway, these bikers work for months. They practice pacing themselves."

Gaby thought of the red-faced racer on the silver bike. She hadn't looked as if she'd been pacing herself. She'd looked as if she'd already used up every bit of her strength.

"Let's go to my house and catch the winners on TV." Tina said. "Then we can see my tape of the crash."

As the others left the alley, Jamal hung back. He wrote a quick note that said, "Alex, meet us at Tina's." He watched as Ghostwriter swirled the letters around. Jamal smiled. He knew Ghostwriter would make sure Alex got the message. "Thanks," he whispered, even though he knew Ghostwriter couldn't hear him.

When they got to Tina's, she put on the TV while Gaby and the others made popcorn. Alex showed up just as Tina was yelling, "Guys! Come on! Here's the end of the race!"

The team rushed into the living room just in time to see the winner roll across the finish line.

"It's the girl on the silver bike!" Gaby shouted. "The one I saw coming out of the alley." She couldn't mistake that bike.

The crowd on TV cheered. Race officials surrounded the winner as she got off her bike. As the TV sportscaster made his way toward her, a voice-over announced the news.

"And the winner of the Big Bike Marathon is Sonya Simms."

On the screen Sonya Simms smiled and waved, acting just the way you'd expect a winner to act. She looked beautiful, not even half as sweaty and tired as Ace Chasen, the second-place racer.

"This is the most thrilling day of my life," Sonya said into a microphone. "I'd like to thank all those who made it possible—especially my twin sister, Gwenna."

"That's nice," Gaby said. "Would you ever thank me in public like that, Alex?"

"In your dreams," Alex said, grinning.

"Well, Sonya Simms did win the race," Jamal said. "I guess you couldn't have seen her coming out of the alley, Gaby. I think the judges would have disqualified her for leaving the race."

"I *did* see her," Gaby insisted. "Tina, can we play your tape and see?"

"Sure," Tina said. She took the videotape out of her

camera and put it into the VCR. A moment later they were looking at their block, the firecrackers, and the bike racers piling up. Winnie Slocum went down. Ace Chasen zoomed by. And they saw Sonya Simms, behind everyone, turn her silver racer into the alley.

"Hey, there she goes," Lenni said.

"Now do you believe me?" Gaby asked.

Tina hit the stop button on the VCR. The TV returned to more live coverage of the race, and Tina went into the kitchen to get more popcorn. Gaby followed her then stopped when she saw a newspaper on the kitchen table. It was turned to a page with articles about the race. One of the stories was headlined ACE CHASEN, ORPHAN RACER. She began to read it. It explained how Ace Chasen's entire family had died in a terrible fire. "That's so sad," Gaby murmured.

Frowning, she took the strange note from the alley out of her pocket. She picked up a pencil and began drawing lines between letters. Ghostwriter got the idea, and letters began hopping around as he helped her try to make sense of the note.

Suddenly Gaby saw the hidden message. And she also saw the truth about the race. She wrote a note to Ghostwriter explaining what she suspected.

BY GEORGE, I THINK YOU'VE GOT IT, the ghost wrote back.

Gaby ran back to the living room, waving the note. "I got it!" she crowed. "I got it! I broke the code!"

"It was a message about Ace Chasen trying to win through a dirty trick," Lenni said. "How could it mean anything else?"

On the TV screen a sign had appeared, announcing the first- and second-place winners.

1—SONYA SIMMS
2—ACE CHASEN

Letters began to move around as Ghostwriter sent a message.

ACE HAS NO SIS

"See?" Gaby said, pointing to the screen and waving the note in her hand. "This isn't about dirty tricks. Don't you get it? It's about cheating."

Do you get it? Follow the clues to solve the mystery.

SOLVE IT YOURSELF

1. Write down the names of the racers who were at the midpoint of the race.
2. Cross out the names of anyone who didn't make it out of the crash and continue in the race.
3. Using one of the codes you've read about in this book, decode the message the Ghostwriter team found.
4. Who is cheating? Write down what you think happened!
5. Turn to page 80 and see if you did solve it yourself!

FOLLOW THAT . . . ?

Footprints and tire marks can be very important clues to follow when you're looking for someone or something—especially if you've lost sight of him or her. Most people might not notice these tracks, but a detective on the lookout will. Here's what some of them look like.

Car

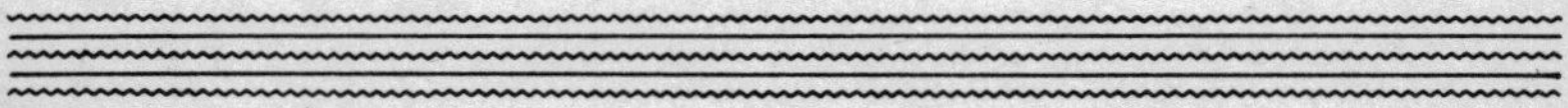

Truck

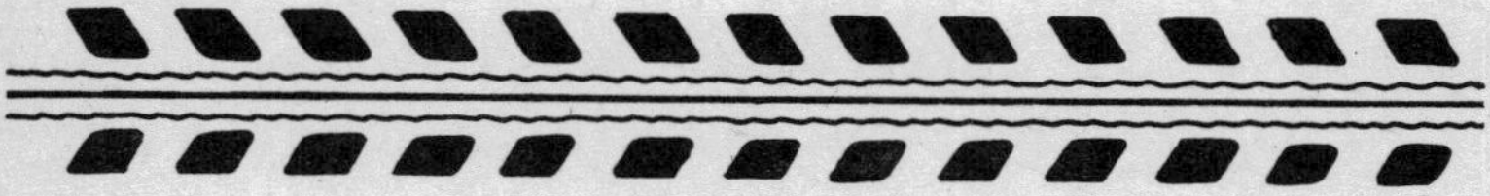

Bicycle

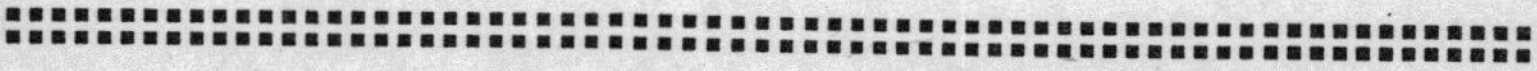

Shoe with heel

Shoe without heel

Sneaker

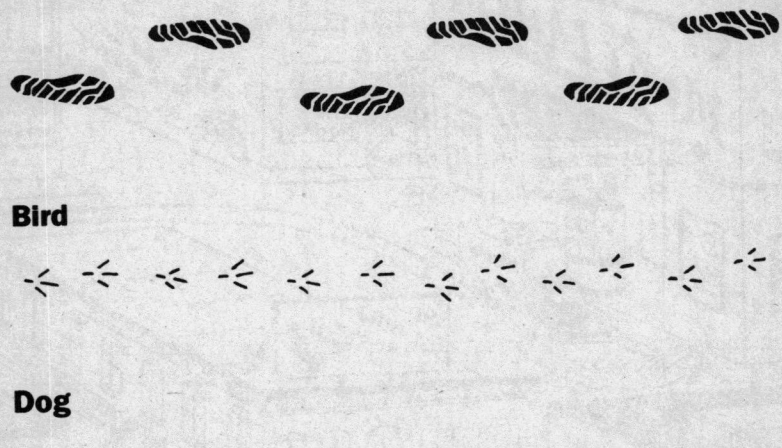

Bird

Dog

FOLLOW THAT GRAFFITI ARTIST

Now turn the page and track down a mysterious graffiti artist in our neighborhood.

If you follow the clues he wrote on the building walls, you'll uncover his secret hiding place. Once you think you've found him, hold the page up to the light to see if you're right.

Start at **Lucy's Gas Station**

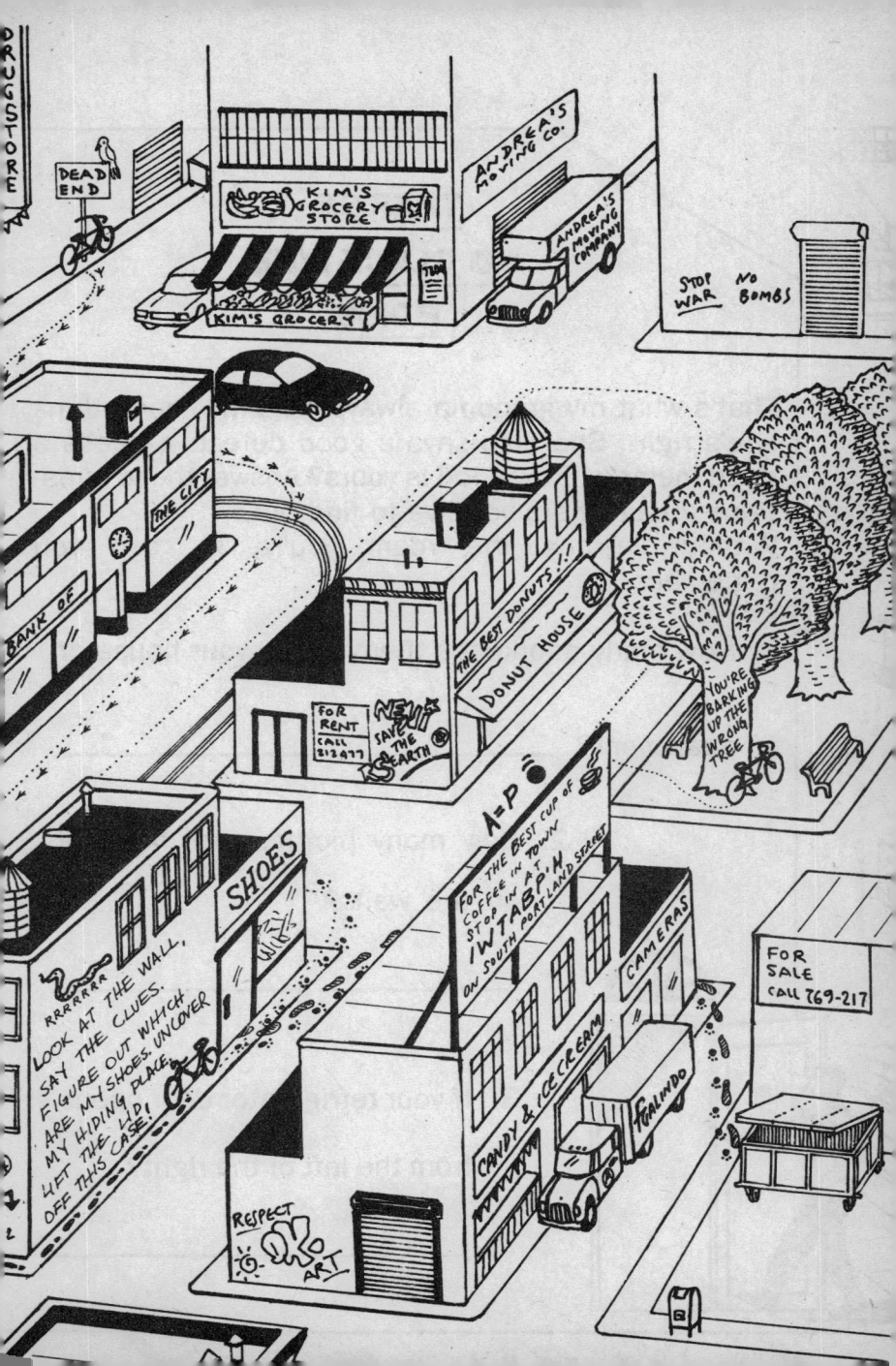

THERE'S
NO PLACE LIKE
HOME

That's what my grandma always tells me, and I think she's right. She also says a good detective needs a good memory! How good is yours? Answer these questions about where you live to find out.

Without leaving the room you're in, can you remember . . .

1. How many doorknobs there are in your house or

   apartment? _____

2. How many pictures are hanging

   on the walls?

   _____

3. If your refrigerator door opens

   from the left or the right?

   _____

4. How many cabinets there are in your kitchen?_____

5. If the key to your front door turns to the left or right when you unlock the door? _____

6. How many drawers are in the room where you sleep? _____

7. How many pillows are in your house or apartment? _____

8. How many closets and windows? _____

SCORE: Answered all 8? Congratulations, Detective *Homes*!
Answered 6 out of 8? Okay! You've made the *Home* team.
Answered less than 4? Hey! Is anybody home?

LENNI'S LOGIC

Even though I've never met any of the shoppers in the bodega on the next page, I know who their families are. How? Each shopper has a cart full of *evidence*.

Look in each cart and you'll be able to match the shoppers to their families. Then write down the evidence you found in each cart on the evidence list below!

EVIDENCE	EVIDENCE	EVIDENCE
Shopper #1 belongs to family:	Shopper #2 belongs to family:	Shopper #3 belongs to family:
A B C?	**A B C?**	**A B C?**
Circle one.	Circle one.	Circle one.
List evidence:	List evidence:	List evidence:

WHERE'S WINSTON?

Mr. Braithwaite, our neighbor, has lost his dog. Can you help us find him by following these *clues*?

Which store is Winston hiding in?
Read each sweet clue below.
Chew over all the facts you see,
And then we're sure you'll know...

Which dog is Winston!

CLUES

1. Look for a woman eating a vanilla ice cream cone.
2. She is next to a girl who is eating a doughnut.
3. This girl is next to a man who is munching on a cookie.
4. He is also holding a lollipop.
5. Winston is hiding in the store behind this group of people!

Winston is hiding in _____

BUY THE DAILY POST
VISIT YOUR LOCAL
CTLHHIPCS

A = P

COHEN'S ICE CREAM

MAX'S DELI

THE CASE OF THE
SHOCKING-PINK ENVELOPE

Grandma's out of the house each day delivering mail. But I know where I can find her if I need her. I just go to the Fernandezes' bodega between 12:00 and 12:30. She'll be there for her lunch break, a coffee cup in one hand and her mail cart right beside her.

I went to find Grandma today because I couldn't figure out how to tell Dad I didn't want to go fishing with him next week. I really like hanging with my dad, but I really hate fishing. It's so slow! Also, I kind of feel sorry for the fish, flapping around on the bottom of the boat trying to escape. One time I helped them. Dad wasn't very happy.

Anyway, when I got to the bodega, Grandma was having lunch with her friend Mr. Braithwaite. Mike Edels, the delivery boy, and Mr. Fernandez were there too. So was Alex. I started talking to him about going to Lenni's birthday party that afternoon.

All in all, it seemed like a normal day. Who would have guessed that my visit to the bodega would send me on a fishing trip. Fishing for a thief, that is!

—from Jamal's journal

"Lenni always gets great presents," Alex said. "Remember last year? Her aunt sent her a brand-new fifty-dollar bill."

"Right," Jamal agreed. "She sends Lenni money every year—always in a bright pink envelope." He laughed. "And she always tells her to put it in the bank for a rainy day."

Just then Willie Boylan stepped from behind a stack of cans carrying some dog food. Willie was a big, husky fourteen-year-old who wasn't known for being nice. "Quit blocking the way!" he growled.

He was so busy pushing past the boys that he didn't notice Grandma Jenkins's mail cart. "Yow!" he yelled as he stumbled over it, bumping into Jamal's grandmother.

Grandma Jenkins fell one way. Her coffee cup flew another way. And her mail cart tipped over and fell in a third direction, knocking over the cupcake rack. Mr. Braithwaite's dog Winston barked and lunged for the spilled cupcakes.

"Hey, Winston! Ho, dog!" called Mr. Braithwaite. But by the time he got that big dog under control, cupcakes and envelopes were scattered all around the store.

Alex and Jamal tried to help his grandmother up. "I think I hurt my ankle," she said. Mr. Fernandez and Mike Edels came out from behind the counter to help them.

Mike picked up the cupcake rack and put it back in place. Then he started picking up the scattered mail. While Mr. Fernandez, Alex, and Jamal checked out Grandma's ankle, Willie stood around complaining. "Hey, I'm ready to pay!" he said.

"How about less griping and more help," Alex muttered.

Mr. Fernandez looked at Willie. "You should also apologize to Mrs. Jenkins," he suggested.

"Okay, okay, sorry." Willie picked up some cupcakes and put them back on the rack. But he was doing it wrong. He put pink strawberry cupcakes beside yellow lemon cupcakes. Jamal didn't get it. Anybody could see that the yellow cupcakes should be in one section and the pink ones in another.

"If you're going to stack those cupcakes, please do it right." Mr. Fernandez sounded a little annoyed at Willie. "Put the strawberry cupcakes with the other pink ones. The lemon cupcakes go with the other yellow ones."

Willie looked a little nervous as he picked up another package of pink strawberry cupcakes. He fumbled for a second. Then he put it with the yellow ones.

Mr. Fernandez scowled. "Willie, please. Stack them right, or don't do it at all."

"Who cares if they're pink or yellow?" Willie snapped. "They're just stupid cupcakes."

"I'll stack the cupcakes, Mr. Fernandez," Mike said, standing up. He had both hands full of letters, which he put back in Grandma Jenkins's mail pouch. "You can pick up the rest of the mail," he said to Willie.

Just then a stranger walked into the store. "What a mess," he said, kneeling to help pick up envelopes. Jamal noticed he was holding a Brooklyn street map.

"I'm lost," he said. "Can you tell me how to get to Myrtle Avenue?"

Mike gave the man directions as they finished picking up the mail. The stranger thanked him and left.

By then Jamal's grandmother was taking a few careful steps. "Well, my dignity may be a little beat-up, but I think my ankle is all right," she said. She pinched Jamal's cheek. "See you later, baby. I'd better get back to work." She went to the mail cart, then stopped. "Where's Lenni's mail?" she asked. "The Fraziers' loft is the next stop on my route."

She went through every letter in her cart. Then she went through them again. "I had two envelopes in here for Lenni—and one was a special delivery."

"In a bright pink envelope?" Jamal asked.

"Shocking pink," Grandma Jenkins answered, nodding. "But now I can't find it—or the one in the light blue envelope, either." She looked worried. "They must still be on the floor somewhere."

Jamal was about to start looking on the floor when he caught a glimpse of a newspaper that was lying on the checkout counter. The letters on the page were scrambling around.

Jamal nudged Alex, then nodded at the newspaper. "Ghostwriter!" he whispered.

Slowly the letters settled into a message from the ghost. "DARLING LENNI," it said. "ANOTHER YEAR OLDER AND MORE BEAUTIFUL THAN EVER!"

"Whoa," Alex whispered. "Ghostwriter must be

reading those words from one of Lenni's letters. That means they're still here somewhere."

Ghostwriter was making another message. This one said: "DEAR LENNI, HAPPY BIRTHDAY. PUT THIS AWAY FOR A RAINY DAY."

Jamal grabbed a pen. He knew Ghostwriter couldn't see where the letters were, but maybe there was a way to figure it out.

"Ghostwriter," he wrote. "We need to find Lenni's letters. Do you see any other words near the letters?"

There was a pause. Then the letters on the newspaper started moving again. Ghostwriter's new message read: "LIBERTY. IN GOD WE TRUST. 1985."

"What is he talking about?" Alex asked.

Jamal stared at the strange message. Something about it was familiar to him. He knew he'd seen it before somewhere.

Then suddenly he knew where. Grinning, he reached into his pocket and pulled out a quarter. "Look," he said to Alex. He pointed to the words engraved around the picture of George Washington. " 'Liberty. In God we trust,' " he read aloud.

"What was that, Jamal?" Grandma Jenkins asked. She, Mr. Fernandez, and Mr. Braithwaite were still searching the bodega for Lenni's two letters.

"Uh, nothing, Grandma," Jamal said quickly. He waited until she had turned away, then he grabbed Alex's arm. "Lenni's letters are near a quarter," he whispered. "Do you know what that means?"

"Yeah," Alex said. He looked worried. "It means

Lenni's letters are in someone's pocket. It means someone stole them."

Jamal nodded. "The question is, who?"

After a while Alex said, "There's something else I don't get. We all know why someone would steal Lenni's pink envelope."

"Because it has all that cash inside," Jamal put in.

"Right," Alex said. "But Ghostwriter says *both* of Lenni's letters are together in someone's pocket. What I want to know is, why did the thief steal both? Why not just take the pink one?"

Alex and Jamal were both stumped. Jamal wrote a quick note filling Ghostwriter in on everything that had happened. Then, hoping that Ghostwriter could help them, he wrote: "What do you think? Why were both letters stolen?"

Some of the letters shifted on the page. "NO IDEA," Ghostwriter wrote back.

Jamal looked around the store. Then, suddenly, he knew. He was staring right at the most important clue—a clue Ghostwriter couldn't find because he could only read things, not see them.

"Mr. Fernandez," Jamal asked, "do you have a dictionary?"

"Yes, I do," Mr. Fernandez said, looking puzzled. "It's on the shelf under the cash register."

Alex reached down and pulled out the dictionary. He handed it to Jamal. Jamal looked up the word *color*. Here's what he found:

col·or-*n* A hue as contrasted with black, white, or gray.
col·or·a·tion-*n* 1 a: the state of being colored > b: use or choice of colors
col·or blind *adj* 1: unable to see colors 2: unable to tell the difference between colors
col·or·cast-*n* : a television broadcast in color

Jamal shut the book with a bang. "You can stop looking, Grandma. I know where Lenni's letters are," he said.

Jamal knows who stole the envelopes. Do you? Follow the clues to solve the mystery.

<u>SOLVE IT YOURSELF</u>

1. Write down the names of everyone who was in the bodega when the mail cart spilled. These are your suspects!
2. Cross out the names of any suspect who did *not* pick up scattered mail.
3. Cross out the suspects who didn't know about Lenni's party and the shocking-pink envelope.
4. Look at the remaining suspects. Why would one of them have to steal both envelopes? *Hint: The clue is in the cupcakes!*
5. Circle the name of the thief. Then write down how you came to your conclusions.
6. Turn to page 80 and see if you did solve it yourself!

FINGERPRINTS: HANDS ON!

I can show you how to pick up the most handy clues around: fingerprints!

You'll need the paintbrush, lead pencil and sandpaper, talcum powder, roll of tape, and scissors from your Ghostwriter Detective Kit.

First find a print you want to lift. The best places to look for fingerprints are on flat, smooth surfaces, such as walls, glasses, tabletops, car doors, paper, and envelopes. If the print is on a dark surface, you'll need your talcum powder to make it show up. If it's on a light surface, grab your pencil—it's time to make lead powder!

Hold the pencil over a piece of paper. Then run some sandpaper or a nail file over the side of your pencil point. You'll see lead powder fall onto the paper. Pour the powder into a container.

1. Pour

Now that you have your fingerprint powder, pour some of it over the print you want to lift. Remember, light powder for dark surfaces and dark powder for light surfaces.

2. Dust

Use the paintbrush to dust the powder lightly from side to side over the print. Cover a wide area around the print. Then gently brush the loose powder away from the print.

3. Press

Press some clear tape carefully onto the powdered print. Cut the tape. Press the tape firmly over the print, rubbing your fingernail over it. Now you'll see the pattern of the powder on the tape.

4. Peel

Peel off the tape carefully, and the print will come up with it. It will show up again when you stick the tape down on a piece of paper. Be sure to use light paper for dark-powdered prints and dark paper for light-powdered ones.

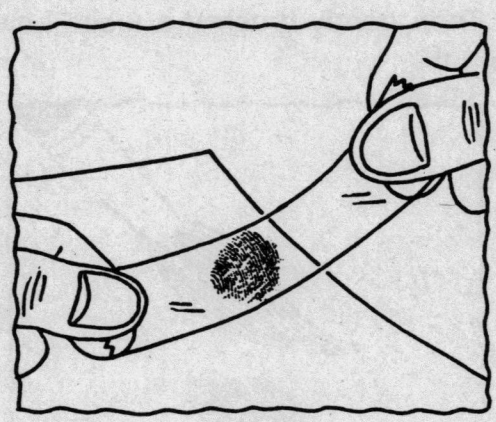

Now you know what it takes to lift fingerprints, and it's as easy to remember as *1 2 3 4*! Write down the four steps here.

1. P _____

2. D _____

3. P _____

4. P _____

FINGERPRINTS: HANDY GUIDELINES

The lines in fingerprints are a detective's best friend and a crook's worst enemy. So let's put the finger on some facts about these fabulous clues.

As far as anyone knows, no two fingerprints in the world are alike. That's why criminals whose fingerprints are on file with the police department are easy to trace. If they leave prints at the scene of a crime, the police can identify them by checking their files and making a match. Even identical twins have completely different fingerprints. And your fingerprints never change—they stay the same as you grow older.

There Are Four Types of Fingerprints . . .

The Arch
The shape in the middle looks like an arch.

The Loop
The shape in the middle looks like a loop. Whenever you see a loop, you'll find a pattern called a *delta*. The delta is where the loop pattern ends.

The Whorl

The shape in the middle is a pattern of lines in a circle. This circle is called a *whorl*. A whorl always has a delta on each side.

Mixed

A mixed print is a combination of different types of fingerprints. There are many kinds of mixed prints. One of the most common is the double loop.

Making a Match...

Decide what type of fingerprint you're looking at: arch, loop, whorl, or mixed. Then see if you can spot any special marks, like a scar or a sudden break in a line. Next, match up the deltas and any other shapes you find. Then count the lines between the deltas and these shapes to see if the number is the same.

Now match my fingerprint to one of the prints below!

1

2

3

4

YOUR FINGERPRINT FILE ALBUM

Keep a fingerprint file. Record your fingerprints right here. Try fingerprinting your friends on a separate piece of paper.

1. Roll the finger you're going to print from side to side on an inkpad.
2. Press the finger very firmly on the paper in this book and roll it from side to side again.

YOUR NAME

LEFT HAND

THUMB   1   2   3   4

RIGHT HAND

THUMB   1   2   3   4

LEFT HAND

THUMB   1   2   3   4

RIGHT HAND

THUMB   1   2   3   4

Now that you've made some prints, you can play . . .

GABY'S GUESSING GLASS GAME

What You Need:

- Three touchy friends! (Two of them must be in your Fingerprint File Album)
- A drinking glass
- Your detective kit's fingerprint powder, tape, scissors, and magnifying glass

How to Play:

1. Have your friends choose one person from the group. Don't let them tell you who it is! Whoever is chosen should touch the glass and leave a clear print on it—after *you* leave the room.
2. Return to the room. Look for the print with your magnifying glass. Then pour, dust, press, and peel the print off the glass.
3. Press the print down on a piece of paper. Now match it to one of the prints in your album. If you simply can't make a match, then it belongs to the friend you haven't fingerprinted yet!
4. Start again with a clean glass—and ask one of your friends to leave the room and give it a try!

SEVEN STEPS AT THE SCENE OF THE CRIME

Whenever I'm at the scene of a crime,
I know what to do if I rap this rhyme.

1.
Look. Don't touch. For good detection,
circle the room in one direction.
2.
Collect fingerprints as you circle again.
3.
Write in your notebook: Who, Where, and When.
4.
Gather your evidence. Bag and label each clue.
5.
Question the victims and witnesses too.
6.
Look around again for evidence.
7.
Work out a story: Use common sense.

Jamal took the pictures on the following pages while we were investigating a break-in at the Party Animal, a party-favor store owned by Mr. and Mrs. Ferguson. The pictures are all mixed up, but you can put them in order by following my rap. I did the first one for you!

What do *you* think happened at the Party Animal? Fill in the blanks to help me work out a story.

Sometime last night on Sunday, December _____,

a crook threw a _____ through the glass win-

dow of the _____ _____ at the Party

Animal. Then he or she entered. It looked like the

crook was someone wearing _____ from the

_____ I found in the spilled glitter. The crook

probably knocked the glitter over when he or she

opened the _____. He or she probably left

through the _____ _____ , as shown

by the direction of the _____ in the glitter.

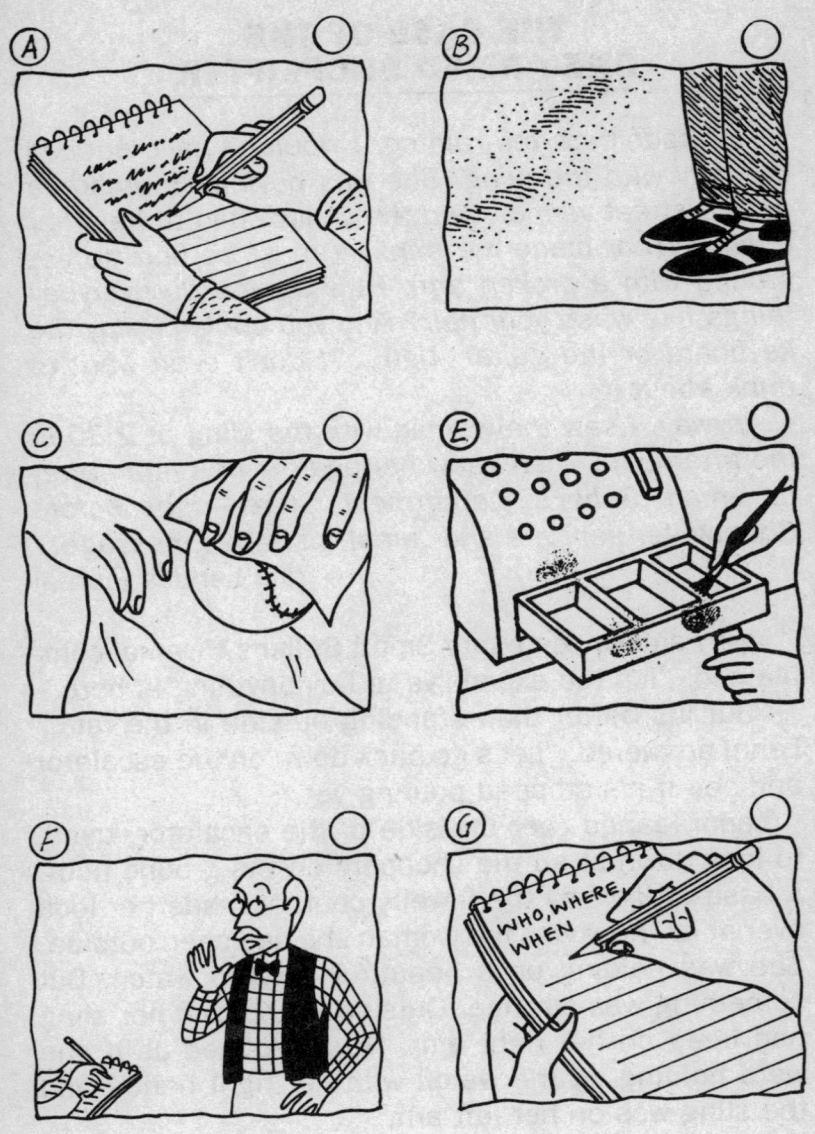

THE CASE OF THE
ONE-ARMED SHOPLIFTER

If it hadn't started raining, I wouldn't have noticed the lady with the sling. She was buying an umbrella from a street vendor, and the vendor had to help her open it. That made me think. It must be hard to get around with a broken arm. How do you do everyday things like wash your hair? And you couldn't play the keyboard or the guitar. Ugh . . . I don't even want to think about it.

Anyway, I saw the woman with the sling at 2:30 in the afternoon. Then I saw her again a half hour later, in Smart Seller's Department Store—right before Ghostwriter sent me and Jamal a strange message!

—from Lenni's journal

"Why did we come into Smart Seller's?" Jamal complained. "It's too expensive to buy anything in here."

"But it's better than standing outside in the rain," Lenni answered. "Let's go back down on the escalator and see if it's stopped pouring yet."

Lenni leaned over the side of the escalator, trying to look down at all the shoppers on the ground floor. A flash of light by the jewelry counter made her look over at it. There was the woman she had seen outside. She was holding up a beautiful jeweled watch. But something was strange. Outside in the rain her sling had been on her right arm. Now it looked as if she were holding up the watch with her right hand—and the sling was on her left arm.

"Psst!" Lenni hissed to Jamal. "There's something very weird about that woman with the sling! Let's keep an eye on her."

Watching from a moving staircase isn't easy. But Lenni and Jamal tried to observe the lady with the sling. She was talking to a young blond salesgirl at the jewelry counter. She kept holding up the watch and turning it, making the jewels flash.

As they got near the ground floor, Lenni looked up at the message painted over the escalator. It said:

Closing Time: 9:00 P.M.

Suddenly some of the letters began to glow with a golden light. It was a message from Ghostwriter, and it said:

LOSING TIME

"Look!" Jamal whispered. He pointed to the sign.

Lenni read her watch. The time was correct. What did Ghostwriter mean? But she didn't have time to pull out her notebook and ask him. The woman with the sling was walking away!

By the time Lenni and Jamal pushed through the crowd to the jewelry counter, the woman with the sling was nowhere in sight. Lenni looked around for the blond salesclerk, but now there was no one behind the counter. As she stood there, she admired the display of beautiful watches. They were very expensive. Several had diamonds set in place of the numbers.

"Wouldn't one of those be nice to have?" Lenni asked.

"Mine isn't as fancy," Jamal said, showing Lenni the watch on his wrist. "But it still tells the time—it's 3:05 on the dot."

Lenni looked at the fancy watches again and noticed that one box was empty.

"Those are *very* expensive watches," a voice said.

Lenni looked up. It was a saleslady—but not the one she'd seen from the escalator. This saleslady had black hair pulled into a tight bun. She looked disapprovingly at Jamal and Lenni.

"These kids aren't going to buy a watch! How about giving *me* some service here?" a raspy voice said. A big man in a damp black raincoat pushed past Lenni and Jamal. His big black shoes nearly crushed Lenni's feet. The man looked like a prizefighter. He had a nose that had once been broken, and his graying red hair was cut very short in a crewcut. A spicy smell hung around him, like the after-shave Lenni's father wore—one of her favorite smells.

"I just noticed that someone must have bought one," Lenni said. "There's an empty box in there."

"What?" The saleslady peered at the empty box. "I just got here. Let me check the sales slips."

But when she looked at the sales slips, the saleslady gasped loudly. "No, that watch has *not* been sold today! Oh, my goodness!"

"I'm not going to stand around here all day!" the nasty man grumbled. He walked away.

A red-haired saleslady leaned over from the perfume counter next to the watch display. "But, Mr. Gabbe, what about your after-shave lotion?" she called after the nasty man.

But he didn't answer. He just kept walking.

Meanwhile the saleswoman at the jewelry counter was punching a number on the telephone. "You children stay right where you are," she said to Lenni and Jamal in a frightened voice.

"You got it," Lenni said. She had the feeling the saleslady thought she and Jamal might have taken the watch. That bothered her. But even so, she had no intention of going anywhere. Not when it looked like there was a mystery going on.

Luckily, when the manager came over, Lenni recognized him. His name was Mr. Percy. He was a fan of her dad's music. Lenni had seen him at a few of Max Frazier's jazz concerts.

It was a good thing too. Otherwise that nervous saleslady would have had Lenni and Jamal arrested for stealing the watch. The woman was so upset, she couldn't think straight. She even started to cry.

"Oh, Mr. Percy," she moaned. "I feel so horrible. It's all my fault! I broke a heel on the subway. So I stopped off and bought an inexpensive pair of sneakers. Then it started to rain, and . . . and I got here five minutes late. If I had been on time, the watch would never have been stolen! It's all my fault!"

"It's not your fault at all, Jane. We've had a rash of shoplifting lately." Mr. Percy shook his head. "That's the second watch this month. The thief must be a real professional. I don't even know where to begin."

Lenni knew where to begin! She wanted to investigate the scene of the crime as soon as she could. There was a suspect—the lady with the sling—and Lenni wanted to see if she had left any fingerprints. "Uh, Mr. Percy," she began. "Maybe I can help."

After Lenni explained what she had in mind, Mr. Percy gave her and Jamal permission to collect any evidence they could find.

First Lenni looked around the counter at the spot where the woman with the sling had stood. She saw fresh sneaker prints, a strand of red hair, and a damp umbrella. Lenni recognized that umbrella. It was the one the lady with the sling had bought from the vendor.

Lenni got out her fingerprint kit. While she was dusting the glass counter with fingerprint powder, she noticed something else—the smell of perfume in the air. More evidence! Eagerly, she brushed and pressed and peeled off fingerprints. She put the red strand of hair in a small envelope and labeled it.

As she did this, Jamal wrote down all the facts—including "strong perfume in the air." He kept his pen out, ready to question any witnesses.

First Jamal planned to question the nervous saleslady. But when he turned around to ask her his first question, she was gone! When Lenni and Jamal found Mr. Percy, he told them that the woman had gone home, too upset to work.

"Jane has been with us for ten years. She deserves an extra day off," he said.

Lenni asked if they could talk to the other jewelry salesclerk.

"You mean Sally Molter?" Mr. Percy shook his head. "Sal clocked out at three P.M. sharp."

So the young salesgirl's name was Sally. Jamal wrote down, "Question Sally Molter later. Ask if she's ever seen the lady with the sling before today."

Lenni took Jamal's pad to draw a map of the scene of the crime. She labeled the wall behind the counter Mirror. Next to it she wrote "Saw lady with sling here. Sling was on the left arm! Before, it was on her right arm. Very suspicious."

As she finished writing, Jamal spotted Ghostwriter trying to ask them something. The ghost began moving all the letters around in a display sign that said:

What a Bonus! It's a Great Buy!
Real Perfection Perfume

When Ghostwriter was done, it read:

WHAT ABOUT THE REFLECTION?

Lenni stared at the message. Then she got it.

"Of course!" she said. "Reflection! The woman with the sling hadn't changed arms after all. I only *thought* she had, because I had seen her reflection in the mirror."

"Then she's not a suspect?" Jamal asked.

Lenni shook her head. "I don't think so. She still could have stolen the watch."

As they stood by the counter, the smell of all those perfumes was so strong they could hardly think.

"It's a good thing Ghostwriter has some ideas," Jamal said. "Look over there."

Ghostwriter was moving letters around in a sign above some funny-looking perfume bottles. He changed

Toot Sweet! The Hot Perfume in a Horn!
to
TRAP THAT THIEF!

"That's a good idea!" Lenni said to Jamal. "We'll stake out the counter and catch the thief."

When they told Mr. Percy about their plan, he liked it. While Lenni and Jamal hid a few feet away, Mr. Percy pretended to be busy putting up signs that said:

Smart Seller's Year-End Jewelry
Sales! Ladies' Watches—All Styles

Then they waited. But not for long! The lady with the sling came back into the store. Mr. Percy looked up from the jewelry counter and walked to her.

"Oh, no!" Lenni whispered to Jamal. "Doesn't he know anything about trapping crooks? He shouldn't talk to her right away!"

"Hello, dear," the woman said. "I left my new umbrella here."

"Darling!" Mr. Percy answered. "How's your arm?"

"It's Mr. Percy's wife!" Jamal said. "I think you got the wrong suspect, Lenni."

"Here's your umbrella, Mrs. Percy." Lenni handed over the umbrella. As Mrs. Percy took it, Lenni noticed her perfume. It was very light, like spring flowers.

"So much for that trap," she muttered to Jamal.

They waited around a little longer, but nothing happened. Lenni was feeling pretty disappointed as she and Jamal started to leave the store. Then Mr. Percy came running up.

"Another watch is missing!" he said. He looked very upset.

Lenni rushed back to the jewelry counter. Again, she found a strong smell of perfume in the air—and another strand of red hair.

"I'm stumped," she said. "I don't even have a suspect."

Jamal looked just as discouraged. "Maybe we should leave the evidence we found with Mr. Percy," he said.

They went to Mr. Percy's office, but he wasn't there. They sat down to wait for him, and Lenni glanced up at the salesclerks' schedule board on the wall. Here's what she saw:

SCHEDULE BOARD

NAME	Mon.	Tues.	Wed.	Thurs.	Fri.
Jewelry Department					
Ms. Jane Cramer	3–9	3–9	3–9	3–9	3–9
Ms. Sally Molter	10–3	10–3	10–3	10–3	10–3
Perfume Department					
Ms. Regina Smith (new trainee)	10–3	10–3	10–3	10–3	10–3

Suddenly Lenni had an idea. She copied part of the schedule in her notebook. Then she jumped out of her seat. "Let's go back to the scene of the crime."

She looked around the jewelry counter again and re-listed all of the things they'd found out, making checkmarks beside certain points.

Jamal looked puzzled, but Ghostwriter seemed to understand what Lenni was getting at. Certain letters on the big sale sign began to glow. When Ghostwriter was done, the sign looked like this:

SMART S**ELL**ER'S **Y**EAR-EN**D J**EW**ELRY
SALES**! **LAD**IES' WATCHES—ALL S**TY**LES

Lenni nodded. Ghostwriter was thinking just what she was thinking. "Let's go back to Mr. Percy," she said to Jamal. "We'll ask him to get some people together so we can take their fingerprints. I think I know who the thief is."

When Mr. Percy had gotten everyone together, Lenni took a set of fingerprints from the person she suspected. She compared them to the ones at the counter.

They matched!

"I was right," Lenni told Jamal.

"But how did you figure it out?" Jamal wanted to know.

Lenni grinned. "I just followed my nose!"

Do you know who the thief is? Follow the clues to solve the mystery.

SOLVE IT YOURSELF

1. Write down the names of everyone who was near the jewelry counter. These are your suspects.
2. Sneaker prints were found near the counter. Who do you *know* was *not* wearing sneakers? Cross out that name.
3. Lenni and Jamal smelled strong perfume at the scene of the crime. Who do we *know* was *not* wearing strong perfume? Cross out that name.
4. A red hair was found at the counter. Cross out the names of any suspects who do not have red hair.
5. Circle the name of the thief. Then write down how you came to your conclusions!
6. Turn to page 84 and see if you did solve it yourself!

 # GHOSTWRITER'S SECRET MESSAGE

As Jamal, Lenni, Alex, and Gaby walked through the neighborhood, they spotted something wrong. Some of the signs were missing. But I found them— and you can too. They're hidden in this book!

To find the missing signs:

1. Turn back to the page number written on each building or sign in the picture on the next page.

2.  When you see this symbol, you've found the missing sign. But it's in secret code.

3. Use your decoder wheel to decode the sign, following my clues.

4. Write your answer in the blanks in the picture.

Now there's only one more thing left for you to do!

There's a New Detective I Want on the Team!

To find out who it is:

1. Circle the first three letters of each sign you just decoded.

2. Now read what you've circled and you'll have the answer!

ANSWERS

Pages 2—4

Ghostwriter

Page 6

1. Grime doesn't pay
2. Because he didn't have any locks
3. A jeweler sells watches
   A jailer watches cells

Page 8

There's a secret message in this book.
How will you find it? Where should you look?
Read to the end. That's my clue.
Then you'll know just what to do.

Pages 10—12

1. They stepped on a scale and got away (a weigh).
2. His nose
3. In the dark.
4. Use the Split It code: Mysterious Secret Messages!

Page 17

1. Split It code: Watch out. The mailman is a spy.

Page 32

1. Ace Chasen
   Winnie Slocum
   Sonya Simms
2. Cross out Winnie Slocum. She left the race after the crash.
3. Use the Split It code: Hi twin! Here we switch to win the race.
4. The rider on the silver bike at the midpoint of the race was Gwenna Simms—Sonya Simms's twin sister. Gwenna and Sonya switched in the alley, and Sonya Simms finished the race. The person in the raincoat who Gaby saw coming out of the alley was Gwenna—after the switch! Sonya Simms cheated to win the race!

Pages 36—37

For illustrated answer turn to page 82.

Pages 40—41

1-B, 2-C, 3-A

Page 42—43

Winston is hiding in Cohen's Ice Cream Store.

Page 50

1. Mr. Fernandez
   Mr. Braithwaite
   Jamal
   Grandma Jenkins
   Alex

Mike Edels
Willie Boylan
The stranger

2. Cross out everyone except Willie, Mike, and the stranger. They were the only ones who picked up mail.
3. Cross out the stranger. He walked into the store *after* Jamal and Alex talked about Lenni's birthday party and the shocking-pink envelope.
4. The remaining suspects are Mike Edels and Willie Boylan. Willie would have to take both envelopes because he is colorblind. Remember—he couldn't tell the difference between the pink cupcakes and the yellow ones! Therefore, he wouldn't be able to tell which envelope was the *shocking-pink* one with the money in it.
5. Willie Boylan stole the shocking-pink envelope!

Pages 56

Number 3

Page 61

Sometime last night on Sunday, December *16*, a crook threw a *baseball* through the glass window of the *front door* at the Party Animal. Then he or she entered. It looked like the crook was someone wearing *sneakers* from the *footprints* I found in the spilled glitter. The crook probably knocked the glitter over

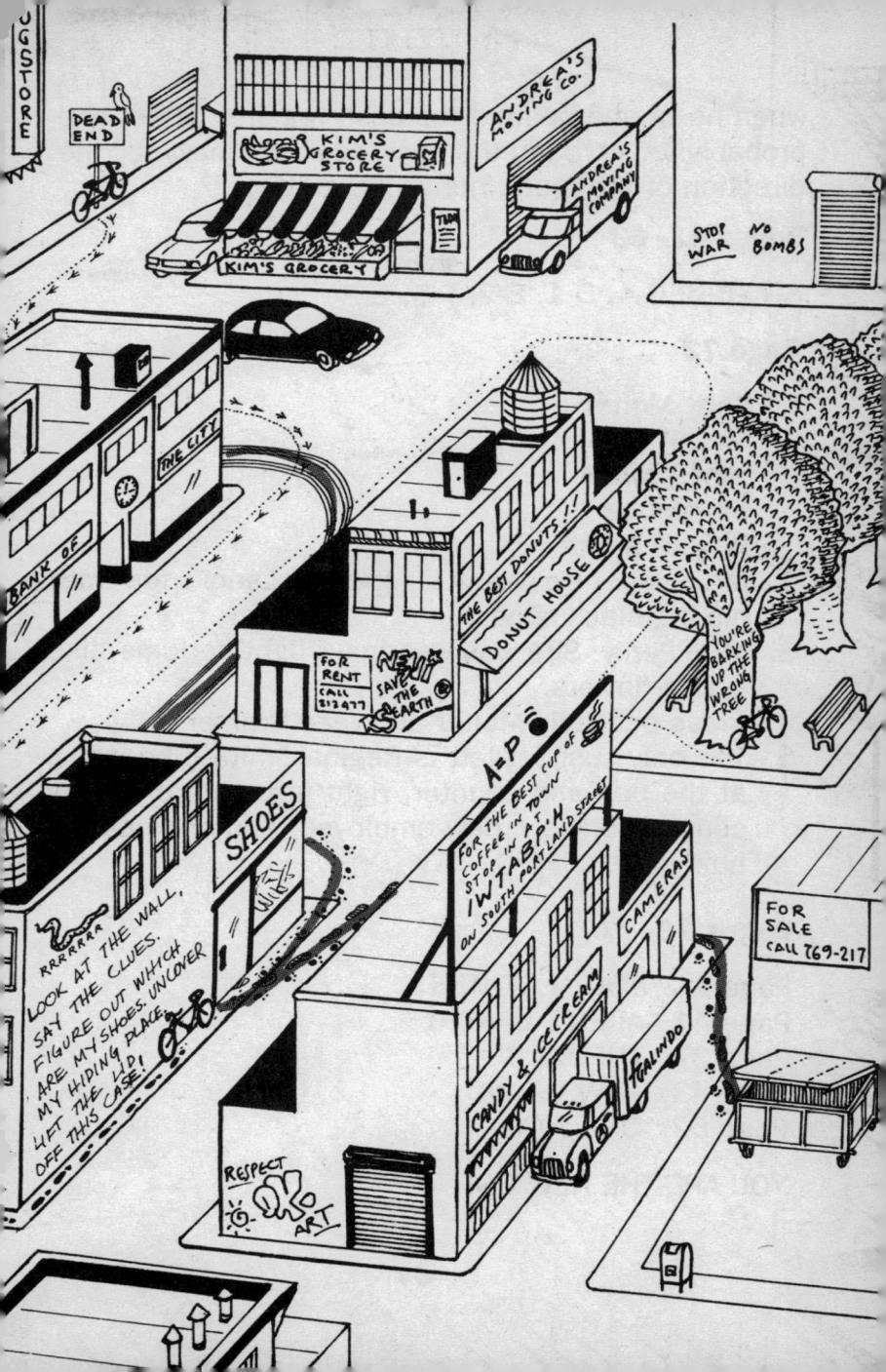

when he or she opened the *cash register*. He or she probably left through the *back door*, as shown by the direction of the *footprints* in the glitter.

Pages 62–63

A-7, B-6, C-4, D-1, E-2, F-5, G-3

Page 73

1. Sally Molter
   Mrs. Percy
   Jane Cramer
   Mr. Gabbe
   Regina Smith
2. Mr. Gabbe. He nearly stepped on Lenni's feet with his big black shoes.
3. Mrs. Percy. She was wearing a light perfume, like spring flowers.
4. Cross out Sally Molter and Jane Cramer.
5. The only suspect left is Regina Smith. She works at the *perfume* counter, right next to the jewelry counter. She's a new employee, and she has red hair!

Pages 76–77

Page 21: YOUTH CENTER
Page 41: AREN'S BAKERY
Page 37: THELMA'S
Page 43: NEWSSTAND
Page 62: ONE WAY

YOU ARE THE NEW ONE

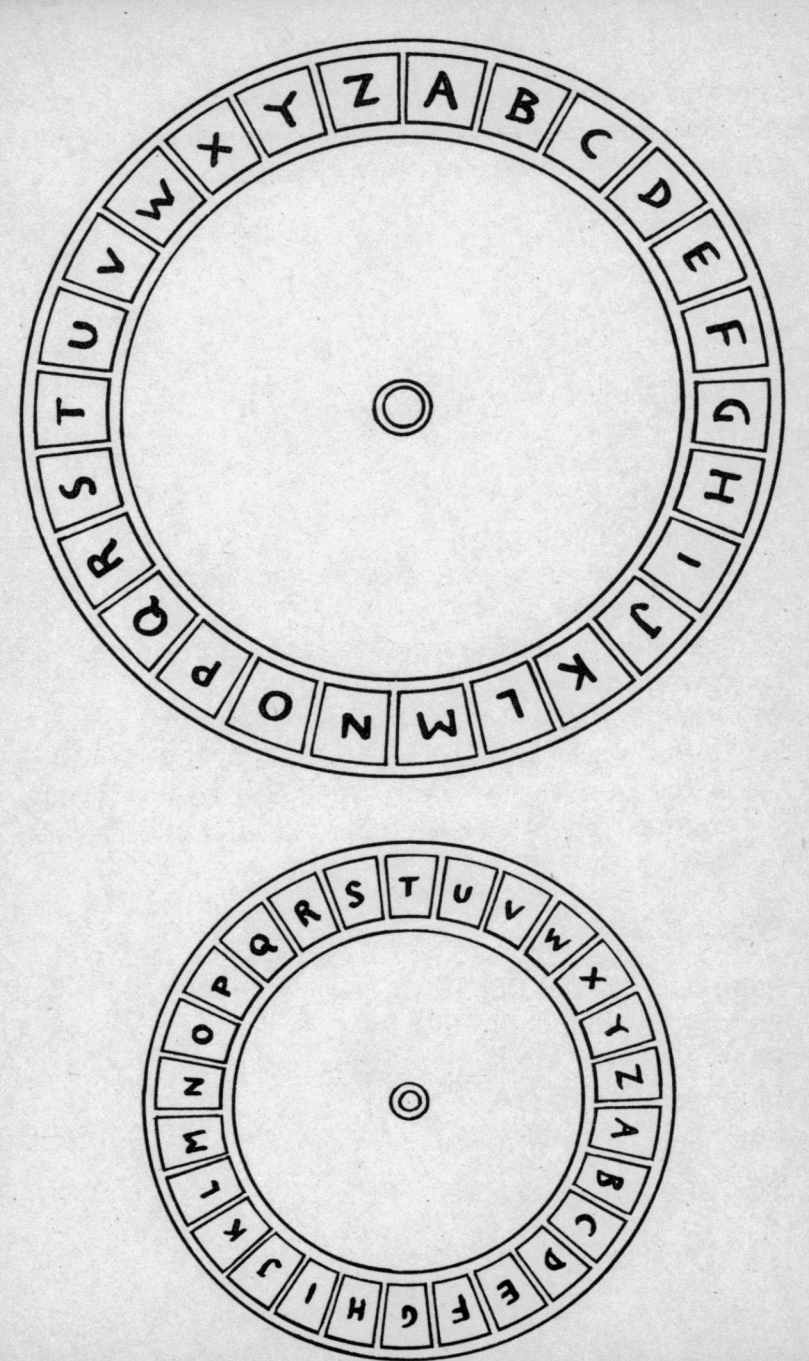

PRESENTING...
two magazines from the people who bring you GHOSTWRITER...

ages **6 to 10**

ages **8 to 12**

KID CITY MAGAZINE
Makes reading, language skills and learning fun. Educates and entertains through stories, puzzles, word games, projects and features. Perfect for Sesame Street Graduates! Ten issues for just $14.97.

3-2-1 CONTACT MAGAZINE
Award winning articles about Nature, Science and Technology. Each issue is packed with puzzles, projects, and challenging Square One TV math pages ...All designed to help your child learn while having fun. Ten issues for just $16.97.

To order the magazine of your choice, send payment to:
Your Magazine Choice
P.O. Box 52000
Boulder, Colorado 80322
(Please allow 5 to 6 weeks for delivery.)

DA53 11/92

MORE FUN-FILLED GHOSTWRITER BOOKS

☐ **A MATCH OF WILLS**   29934-4
by Eric Weiner $2.99/$3.50 in Canada

☐ **THE GHOSTWRITER DETECTIVE GUIDE:**   48069-3
Tools and Tricks of the Trade
by Susan Lurie $2.99/$3.50 in Canada

☐ **COURTING DANGER AND OTHER STORIES**   48070-7
by Dina Anastasio $2.99/$3.50 in Canada

☐ **DRESS CODE MESS**   48071-5
by Sara St. Antoine $2.99/$3.50 in Canada

☐ **THE BIG BOOK OF KIDS' PUZZLES**   37074-X
by P.C. Russell Ginns $1.25/$1.50 in Canada

☐ **THE MINI BOOK OF KIDS' PUZZLES**   37073-1
by Denise Lewis Patrick $.99/$1.25 in Canada

Bantam Books, Dept DA55, 2451 South Wolf Road, Des Plaines, IL 60018
Please send me the items I have checked above. I am enclosing $ _____ (please add $2.50 to cover postage and handling). Send check or money order, no cash or C.O.D's please.

Mr/Mrs _____

Address _____

City/State _____ Zip _____

Please allow four to six weeks for delivery.
Prices and availability subject to change without notice.   DA55 11/92

From the Hit TV Show

GHOST writer

Created by CTW

BECOME AN OFFICIAL
GHOSTWRITER READERS CLUB MEMBER!

You'll receive the following GHOSTWRITER Readers Club Materials:
Official Membership Card • The Scoop on GHOSTWRITER •
GHOSTWRITER Magazine

All members registered by December 31st will have a chance to win
a FREE COMPUTER and other exciting prizes!

OFFICIAL ENTRY FORM

Mail your completed entry to: Bantam Doubleday Dell BFYR,
GW Club, 1540 Broadway, New York, NY 10036

Name

Address

City   State   Zip

Age   Phone

★

"If you really want to be a good attacker," Tess told Yasmine, "you need to learn how to read the field and control the ball—"

"Speaking of controlling the ball, look at Sarah," Nicole interrupted.

Tess saw her teammate on the field, trying to juggle a ball with her knees. Her clumsy attempts made Tess feel a little depressed. With players like that, the Stars would never win a game.

"Forget about reading the field," Nicole said. "If you really want to score, you should figure out a way to get rid of beginners like Sarah."

"Nicole!" Yasmine looked shocked.

Nicole patted Yasmine on the back. "I'm just kidding. Come on, let's go warm up and see if we can help Sarah out."

Nicole and Yasmine trotted off to join Sarah.

But Tess hesitated for a moment before following them. The conversation had given her an idea. . . .

Foul Play

by

Emily Costello

A SKYLARK BOOK

NEW YORK · TORONTO · LONDON · SYDNEY · AUCKLAND

RL 5, 008–012

FOUL PLAY

A Bantam Skylark Book / May 1998

Skylark Books is a registered trademark of Bantam Books, a division of Bantam Doubleday Dell Publishing Group, Inc. Registered in U.S. Patent and Trademark Office and elsewhere.

ISBN 0-553-48644-6

Published simultaneously in the United States and Canada

Bantam Books are published by Bantam Books, a division of Bantam Doubleday Dell Publishing Group, Inc. Its trademark, consisting of the words "Bantam Books" and the portrayal of a rooster, is Registered in U.S. Patent and Trademark Office and in other countries. Marca Registrada. Bantam Books, 1540 Broadway, New York, New York 10036.

PRINTED IN THE UNITED STATES OF AMERICA

OPM   0   9   8   7   6   5   4   3   2   1

for Amelia Elizabeth Costello

GEENA DI GREGORIO'S BIG BROWN EYES scanned the faces of the girls standing on the side of the soccer field. The Stars—an American Youth Soccer Organization team in Beachside, Michigan—were practicing for the first time that afternoon.

I don't know anyone, Geena thought, her stomach giving a nervous twist. Geena went to a small Catholic school a few miles outside Beachside, so she wasn't surprised that she didn't know any of the Stars.

Geena ignored her nervousness and squared her shoulders. *You joined this team to meet new people,* she reminded herself. *So go meet some!*

The other Stars were standing in groups spread out across the field. Some of the girls looked as nervous as Geena felt. But two girls standing on the side of the field seemed calm and sure of themselves. Geena headed in their direction.

"Excuse me," Geena said, willing her voice to sound confident. "Is this where the Stars are practicing?"

A tall girl with long blond hair gave Geena a friendly smile. "Sure is. My name is Tess. Welcome to the team."

"Thanks!" Geena let out her breath in a rush. Now that she was actually talking to a couple of her new teammates, she felt much better. "Did I miss anything?"

"Not yet." Tess's blue eyes were warm as she poked the pretty African American girl standing next to her. "Our coach hasn't even shown up yet. Right, Tameka?"

"Actually . . . wrong." Tameka wore her hair in dozens of elaborate braids, which were pulled back into a ponytail. "I think she just arrived."

Geena followed Tameka's gaze, and saw a slender woman jogging onto the field. She was wearing cleats and carrying a net bag of soccer balls.

The afternoon sunlight bounced off her shiny auburn hair.

"Hi, everyone!" the woman said. "My name is Marina Santana, and I'm going to be your coach this year. Please come out onto the field and form a circle so that we can all get to know each other."

Geena immediately decided she liked Marina. The coach didn't seem much older than the high-school girls who sometimes baby-sat her little brothers and sisters. And Marina had a nice, friendly smile.

As the girls moved into a circle, Geena found herself standing next to Tess. Tameka was on Tess's other side.

"We're going to pass the ball across the circle," Marina explained. "When the ball comes to you, call out your name and tell us something about yourself. I'll go first."

Marina rested her foot on the ball. "I played soccer for my college, North Carolina State, until I graduated last year," she told the girls. "This fall I started graduate school, where I'm studying sports psychology." When Marina finished, she passed the ball to Tess.

Tess neatly stopped the ball. "My name is Tess

Adams," she said. "And I've been playing soccer since I was five."

Whoa, Geena thought. *I hope I'm not the only beginner on the team.* The only soccer experience Geena had was playing with her little brothers and sisters in their backyard.

Marina grinned. "How many years does that make all together?"

"Six," Tess said.

"Terrific," Marina said.

Geena watched Tess pass the ball across the circle. The ball rolled right between the legs of a tall, strong-looking girl with heavy brown bangs. The girl's eyes widened in horror as she watched the ball roll away.

"What do I do?" she asked.

Marina laughed. "Go get it."

The girl chased after the ball, scooped it up, and carried it back to the circle. Giggling nervously, she put the ball on the ground.

"I'm Sarah Mere," the girl said. "And this is my first season."

Geena gave Sarah what she hoped was a reassuring smile. She was glad there was another beginner on the team.

Sarah kicked the ball, which rolled about halfway across the circle, then hit a lump of soil and came to a stop.

Tameka walked out into the circle. She used her foot to pull the ball back to her spot. "I'm Tameka Thomas," she said. "I love playing and watching soccer. My favorite pro player is Cobi Jones."

"She even wears her hair like he does," Tess chimed in.

Tameka laughed. "Well, you've gotta admit that Cobi's dreads are cool!" she said, confidently passing the ball across the circle.

"I'm Nicole Philips-Smith." A girl with a perfectly styled blond bob stopped the ball without glancing down. "I played on Tameka's team last season."

Geena noticed that Nicole was wearing a hint of pale lipstick and a T-shirt from the Country Day Academy. She knew that was an expensive private school nearby.

Using the inside of her foot, Nicole kicked the ball across the circle. Geena's heart jumped when she realized the ball was heading in her direction—fast! She put out her foot. The ball hit it and bounced up into the air. Without thinking, Geena reached out and grabbed the ball—stopping it just before it smacked her in the face.

Nicole rolled her eyes.

Geena could feel herself flush. *Stupid mistake,* she thought.

"In case any of you don't know," Marina said kindly, "soccer players are not allowed to touch the ball with their hands when the ball is in play."

"The goalkeeper can," Tess said.

"That's true," Marina agreed. "But *only* the goalkeeper."

"Actually, I knew that." Geena didn't want her new teammates to think she was *completely* clueless. She put the ball down quickly and kicked it across the circle without bothering to aim. She was beginning to think taking on a new sport wasn't such a great idea.

The ball rolled toward Marina, who stopped it. "Hang on a minute—you forgot to tell us your name."

"Geena Di Gregorio," Geena mumbled, even more embarrassed. She turned toward Tess. "I guess that was pretty lame."

"Don't worry," Tameka said. "You'll learn fast."

"We can help, if you want," Tess added.

Geena felt a tiny bit better. *At least my team-mates seem nice,* she thought.

Marina passed the ball to a girl with a blond ponytail and bushy eyebrows. She'd tied the bottom of her pink T-shirt in a knot. "Lacey Essex," she said, pointing to herself. "And there's nothing in this world I love more than soccer."

"Except boys," Tameka clarified.

A bunch of the girls giggled, and Geena joined in.

Lacey didn't seem embarrassed. "I like boys too," she admitted. "And my absolute favorite thing is boys who play soccer."

Lacey passed the ball to a girl with pale skin and freckles. The girl wore a baseball cap over her short brown hair. Her shorts hung off her skinny frame.

The girl stopped the ball with a well-worn cleat. "I'm Fiona," she told the others. "Don't freak out if I start to wheeze in the middle of practice. I have asthma and I'm allergic to grass."

"And chocolate," Lacey said. "And peanuts."

Fiona nodded with a smile. "We go to school

together," she explained. "I'm the sneeze queen of Beachside Middle School." She passed the ball.

A girl with long dark hair and olive skin stopped it. "Hi, everyone," the girl said. "My name is Yasmine Madrigal, but call me Yaz."

Yasmine thoughtfully tapped the ball back and forth between her feet. "What else? Oh, I grew three inches this winter. And my goal this season is to score more goals."

"I thought Yago scored the goals and you played defense," Tameka said.

"Who's Yago?" Marina asked.

Yasmine made a face. "My obnoxious twin brother," she explained. "He's playing on the Suns this season."

The Suns were a boys' team in their league, Geena knew. Her brother Peter was on that team.

"Last season, Yago scored something like six times each game," Yasmine continued. "He's been bragging about how great he is all winter. I want to show him he's not the only person in the world who can put a ball in the goal."

"I'll help you," Tess offered.

Marina winked at Tess. "Me too," she said.

"Cool!" Yasmine passed the ball to a girl with

pretty red hair. The girl stopped the ball by awkwardly jumping in front of it.

"I'm Rose O'Connor." The redhead smiled, exposing a tangle of braces. "This is my first time playing soccer. I decided to join a team after seeing a totally awesome pro game in Florence, Italy, while I was there on vacation over Christmas."

Rose passed the ball to Tameka.

Tameka looked surprised. "Um—I already had this," she said.

"Oops," Rose said. "I forgot."

"It's okay." Tameka shrugged and passed the ball to a quiet girl with brown hair. She was wearing a neat pair of shorts and a matching T-shirt. Her thick hair was combed into a perfect French braid.

"I'm Jordan Goldman." The girl was speaking so quietly that the others leaned forward to hear her better. Jordan's face was as red as a tomato.

She sure is shy, Geena thought.

"Um—I like to play defense," Jordan mumbled. "And, er—"

"Jordan and I go to the same school," Rose put in. "We're both in the orchestra. I play violin and Jordan plays piano."

"Right." Jordan shot Rose a thankful look. Then she passed the ball to the last person in the circle.

"My name is Amber Chappel," the girl said. "I think my T-shirt about sums it up." Geena squinted to read the T-shirt in the bright sun— RECYCLE NOW. I'LL SHOW YOU HOW!

"Thanks, everyone. That was great," Marina said after Amber had passed the ball back to her. "Now let's find some shade so that we can have a quick team meeting."

The girls headed toward the sidelines. Geena let Tameka and Tess walk ahead. She fell into step with Rose and Sarah.

"I'm glad I'm not the only beginner on this team," Geena told the others with a big smile.

"Me too!" Rose agreed.

Sarah nodded. "Me three!" she said.

chapter 2

"I CAN'T BELIEVE WE HAVE SO MANY beginners on our team," Tess whispered to Tameka as they followed Marina toward a big oak tree on the side of the field. "Three new players out of eleven. That's really rotten luck."

"I'm sure they'll learn fast," Tameka said. "At least everybody seems nice."

Tess shook her head impatiently. "You think *everyone* is nice," she told Tameka. "You've never met a single person you didn't like."

"That's not true," Tameka said. "I don't like Willow Barnes."

Tess rolled her eyes. Willow had been an awful

girl in their kindergarten class. And Tameka had even liked *her*—until Willow bit her.

Anyway, Tess didn't really care how *nice* her teammates were. She was more interested in how well the other girls played and how seriously they took the game.

Mental attitude was everything, Tess knew. She thought Tameka's laid-back approach to life explained why Tameka had scored only half as many goals as Tess the previous season—even though Tameka played almost as well as Tess did.

I scored more because I play to win, Tess told herself. Tess was always pushing herself to learn new soccer skills. During the off-season, she practiced soccer in her backyard. When it snowed, she moved into the basement. Tess wanted to play on the Olympic team someday, and she was willing to work hard to make her dream a reality.

Marina sat down in the grass under the tree and motioned for the girls to join her.

Tess plopped down next to Tameka.

Marina started to talk, giving the girls an idea of what to expect during the season. "Each and every one of you will get to play at least a half in every game," she concluded after a few minutes.

"And everyone will get a chance to play each position over the course of the season. Those are AYSO rules, and I think they're good ones."

"Do we *have* to play all the positions?" Tess asked, making a face. She thought playing defense was boring.

Marina nodded. "I'm going to be rotating each player through each position."

Not me, Tess thought. She promised herself she would get out of playing defense somehow. She was so good at scoring that her old coach had let her play attacker in every game. *Maybe Marina will do the same thing,* Tess thought hopefully.

"Here's a copy of *The ABCs of AYSO,*" Marina continued. "It will answer a lot of the questions you and your parents may have about our league and the laws of soccer. Please let me know if there is anything you don't understand. Oh—and we still need an assistant coach. If any of your parents are interested, have them call me."

Tess took one of the booklets and flipped through it. She'd mastered the laws of soccer long ago, but this was her first season playing for an AYSO team and she was curious about the organization.

Marina opened a cardboard box. "And here are

your uniforms," she announced. The coach spent the next ten minutes making sure that each player had a pair of yellow shorts and a yellow jersey that fit.

As soon as Tess got her jersey, she pulled it on over the T-shirt she was wearing to show her team spirit. Most of the Stars followed her lead, but Nicole tied her jersey around her waist.

"And these are our schedules." Marina handed each girl a bright blue sheet of paper. "We have practice on Tuesday and Thursday at four, and games each Saturday starting in two weeks. Pay attention on game days. The boys' teams will be playing in the next field, so there will be a lot of people in the area. And try to save some time after the games so that we can go out for ice cream at Tosca's together. My treat."

"You mean after each game we win, right?" Tess asked.

"No," Marina said. "After *every* game. I want you guys to have fun. Don't worry about winning."

"Why would I worry about *winning*?" Tess whispered to Tameka. "It's *losing* I'm worried about!"

★

"Is everyone warmed up?" Marina called out at the Stars' practice on Thursday.

"Yes!" Tess said. She was eager to get to work.

Marina and the team had just spent ten minutes stretching. Meanwhile, Tameka's dad—who had volunteered to be the Stars' assistant coach—had arranged bright orange plastic cones across the field.

"Okay," Marina said. "Today we're going to work on your dribbling skills. The challenge is to maintain control over the ball while you dribble in and out, around these cones. Think about using your foot to direct the ball. Has anyone done this drill before?"

Tess raised her hand.

Marina tossed the ball to her. "Okay, Tess, why don't you go first?"

Tess got control of the ball and dashed off toward the first cone. She dribbled around the cones easily—using the tops, insides, outsides, and bottoms of both feet. Tess pushed herself to finish the drill as fast as possible without letting the ball get away. When she got to the end of the field, she lightly touched the ball with the bottom of her foot to stop it. Then she jumped over the ball, turned around, and started back to the beginning of the course.

"Perfect!" Marina exclaimed when Tess had finished.

"Thanks." Tess was slightly out of breath.

"Okay, who's next?" Marina asked.

The other Stars looked at each other.

"Not me!" Geena said, taking a step backward.

Nicole rolled her eyes. "I'll go."

Tess passed the ball to Nicole and went to stand with Tameka.

"Nice job," Tameka said.

Tess shrugged. "No biggie. I've done that drill about a thousand times in my backyard."

"Still, it's not easy," Tameka said. "Look at Nicole."

Nicole was a decent dribbler. But she kept kicking the ball too hard and losing control of it as she rounded the cones. She had to chase the ball and bring it back to the cones, which slowed her down.

"Not bad," Marina told Nicole when she finished. "But next time, try slowing down a little."

Nicole nodded. She walked over to Tess and Tameka with a satisfied smile on her face. "Practices at the beginning of the season are so boring," she said.

"What do you mean?" Tameka asked.

Nicole gestured in the direction of the cones. "All these baby drills are a drag," she said.

"I don't think so," Tess said. Her eyes were on the field, where Lacey was running through the cones. Lacey's dribbling was smooth and skillful.

"You don't?" Nicole demanded.

Tess shook her head. "Dribbling is crucial to a strong game," she said. "It always pays to practice the basics."

"Maybe if you're a beginner," Nicole said.

"Even if you're a pro," Tess told Nicole. "Besides, your dribbling could definitely use some more work."

"Work?" Nicole's face flushed.

"Yeah," Tess continued. "You're kicking the ball too hard. If you just tap it—"

"I know how to dribble!" Nicole interrupted. "I don't need you to tell me."

"I'm just trying to help," Tess said.

"I don't need your help!" Nicole put her nose in the air and walked over to where Lacey was standing.

Tess blinked in surprise. Nicole's attitude was so . . . *dumb*. How could Nicole improve if she wasn't interested in learning what she did wrong?

"Nicole thinks you were putting down her dribbling," Tameka said.

"I was just being honest," Tess said as she watched Sarah do the drill. "Nicole didn't need to get so defensive."

"Tameka—your turn!" Mr. Thomas called.

While Tameka went off to do the drill, Tess ran over to Sarah, who had just finished.

"Hi." Sarah looked a little surprised to see Tess coming toward her.

"Hi," Tess responded. "I wanted to tell you something. You're dribbling with just the inside of your foot—"

"That's what Marina said too." Sarah sighed. "But I don't really know what she means."

"Can I show you?" Tess asked.

"Sure," Sarah answered.

Tess got a ball and showed Sarah how to dribble the right way.

"Try it," she said, passing the ball to Sarah.

Sarah dashed after the ball and then started to dribble it along the touchline—exactly the same way she had during the drill.

"Use the outside of your foot too!" Tess called.

A few steps later, Sarah touched the ball with the outside of her foot. But the unusual movement threw her off balance. She stumbled and fell hard on her knees.

Tess ran over to Sarah, who was already getting up. "Are you okay?" she asked anxiously. "That was some fall."

"Oh, that was nothing." Sarah brushed off her legs as best she could. There were grass stains on her knees. "My mom always says if you don't need stitches, it isn't that bad."

"What happened?" Tess asked.

Sarah shrugged. "I probably tripped over my own feet. Happens all the time. Should I try some more?"

"Definitely," Tess said. "You seemed to have the hang of it there for a second."

Tess watched as Sarah dribbled down to the end of the field and then turned around and dribbled back toward the others.

"That looks much better," Marina called to Sarah.

Sarah grinned. "Tess showed me what to do."

"Thanks for the help," Marina told Tess.

"You're welcome!" Tess was happy to do whatever she could to help her teammates play better. That way the Stars would have a better chance of winning games.

chapter 3

T HE NEXT TWO WEEKS WERE BUSY ONES. The time flew by, and before Tess knew it, the last practice before the Stars' first game had arrived.

"Okay, guys, let's have a quick scrimmage," Marina said after the Stars had completed a drill.

"Yippee!" Tess gave Tameka a high five. She loved scrimmages—and this was the first one the Stars had played.

"Tess, Tameka, Rose, Jordan, and Nicole, come and get a practice jersey from me," Marina said. "You'll be the blue team. Everyone else, just wear your T-shirts."

Tess ran over to the coach.

Marina pulled the thin jerseys out of a net bag.

She tossed one to each girl. Since the girls were playing with such small teams, they'd use only half the field. Mr. Thomas set up some goals with the cones while everyone got ready.

"I wish Yaz and Lacey were on our side," Tess muttered to Tameka as the girls pulled on their jerseys.

Tameka shrugged. "This is just practice. It's not important to have all the best players on our team."

"It's important if you want to win," Tess argued.

Nicole was standing nearby. "What makes you think we won't win?" she demanded. "I'm a good player too. Better than Lacey or Yaz."

"I didn't mean—" Tameka started to say.

Nicole silenced her with a wave of her hand. "You two think you're the best players on the team. But I'm just as good as you are."

"Yeah—but your attitude stinks," Tess mumbled.

"What did you say?" Nicole demanded hotly.

"Nothing," Tess said.

Nicole gave Tess an angry look and then walked off to join the rest of the girls, who had gathered around Marina and Mr. Thomas.

Over the past week and a half, the Stars had

gotten to know each other better. Tess thought her new teammates were great—except for Nicole. The two seemed to bicker constantly.

Tess sighed as she and Tameka followed Nicole. "Nicole doesn't like me," she said.

"She sure doesn't," Tameka agreed with a little laugh. "I think she may be a tiny bit jealous of you. She was the best player on our team last season."

Tess shrugged. She knew she couldn't be friends with everyone—even if Tameka could—but it still bothered her that Nicole was so nasty to her all the time.

"Okay, guys," Marina said. "We're going to play without a goalkeeper during this scrimmage. Jordan, I want you to play defense near the goal. Nicole and Rose, you'll handle the midfield. That leaves Tess and Tameka as attackers. Does anybody have any questions?"

Rose nodded. "What does a midfielder do?"

"When your team has the ball, try to move it closer to your goal," Marina explained. "You can do that by dribbling it or passing up to the attackers."

"What if the other team has the ball?" Rose asked.

"Then do everything you can to steal the ball from them," Tess said.

"And help me stop them from making a goal," Jordan put in quietly. Now that Jordan knew the other girls better, she was less shy around them.

"Right," Marina agreed. "Any other questions?"

The girls all shook their heads.

"Then line up!" Marina ordered.

Tess fell into step with Rose as they headed onto the field. "If you get the ball during the game, listen to what the rest of us are calling to you," she suggested. "We'll help you figure out who's open."

Rose swallowed hard. "You don't have to do that. . . ."

"It's no problem," Tess said. "It called 'talking it up,' and soccer players always do it."

Rose flashed Tess a metallic grin. "Thanks," she said.

"Sure." Tess smiled back. She ran to stand near Tameka on the front line. She noticed that Marina had assigned Geena and Yasmine to be attackers for the other side.

Marina put the ball down in the middle of the four of them. "Play ball!" she called.

Geena didn't move. She looked a bit confused.

Tess took advantage of the opening. She dashed toward the ball and kicked it out of Geena's reach.

Tameka reacted perfectly. She ran closer to the goal, trying to move away from Yasmine, who was covering her.

Tess started to dribble the ball toward the other team's goal. But Lacey was covering her closely. She kept reaching between Tess's feet, trying to steal the ball.

I need to pass, Tess decided. Rose and Jordan were playing way back near the goal. But Nicole was open.

Well, too bad, Tess thought stubbornly. *I'm not going to pass the ball to Nicole and make her think she's better than I am.*

Instead, Tess passed to Tameka. "Heads up, Tameka!" she yelled.

The pass was good, and Tameka quickly got control of the ball. But a second later, Yasmine stole it away from her.

Yasmine drove toward the blue team's goal. Tameka ran after Yasmine, but she couldn't get in front of her.

"Stop her!" Tess hollered.

Nicole ran forward to challenge Yasmine.

With one player behind her and one in front, Yasmine panicked. She shot the ball toward the goal without even aiming.

Please don't let her score, Tess thought. Her heart soared when she realized that the ball was sailing right toward Rose.

"Way to be there, Rose," Tess shouted. "Stop it with your chest."

Rose saw the ball coming. She made a strangled sound in her throat—and ducked. The ball soared over Rose's head and continued toward the goal.

"Don't be afraid of the ball!" Tess called to Rose. "Control it."

"Sorry," Rose said meekly.

"That's okay," Marina yelled from the sidelines.

Maybe it's okay this time, Tess thought. *But if Rose does that in a game, it could be a disaster.*

Tess watched as Jordan trapped the ball and gave it a strong kick. The ball came down just in front of Nicole. Nicole stopped the ball with her chest and began to drive forward along the left touchline.

Tameka ran into position in front of the goal. "I'm open!" she yelled at Nicole.

But Nicole didn't pass. She continued to drive forward until she was almost parallel with the goal. Then she kicked. The ball rolled slowly across the field.

No, no, no! Tess thought. *Shots on goal should be powerful!* Any halfway-decent goalkeeper could have stopped Nicole's shot with her eyes closed.

Tameka ran forward to give the ball an extra push. But Amber got there first. She stopped the ball, turned it around, and passed to Yasmine.

Yaz drove the ball up the middle of the field and then passed to Lacey, who was open in front of the goal.

Lacey tapped the ball in.

"Yes!" Yasmine shouted, throwing her hands up in the air.

"Goal!" Marina called. "Nice teamwork, Yaz, Amber, and Lacey. Okay, guys, it's almost five o'clock. Let's cool down before we head home."

"Please let us play more," Tess begged.

"Sorry, but not today," Marina said. "Lacey, would you get the ball? Everyone else, let's form a circle. Okay, hinge at your waists. Let your arms hang loose. Keep your knees slightly bent. Feel the pull in your hamstrings."

Yasmine was standing next to Tess. "Why are you frowning?" she asked as the girls hung upside down.

"I wanted to score," Tess said.

"You're just mad because our team won," Yasmine said in a light tone.

Tess didn't laugh. She turned toward Tameka, who was on her other side. "This is all Nicole's fault," she said.

"Tess!" Even upside down, Tameka looked shocked. "Come on. This was just a scrimmage. In a real game, we'll all be on the same side."

"I know," Tess said. "But I hate to lose. Even if it *is* just a scrimmage."

★

"How was soccer practice this afternoon?" Mr. Madrigal asked that evening at dinner. Yasmine's family was gathered around the table in their sunny kitchen.

"Grapf," Yago mumbled.

Yasmine watched in disgust as bread crumbs flew out of her twin brother's mouth. "Yago!" she said. "Don't talk with your mouth full. Besides, Dad was asking *me* about soccer practice. Not you."

"Was not!" Yago shot back.

Mr. Madrigal held up a hand. "Kids—I was talking to both of you."

Yasmine closed her eyes and wished her twin brother would just disappear. But when she opened her eyes, he was still there.

Why couldn't Yago have been my identical twin? Yasmine wondered for about the zillionth time. *That way he would have been a girl, and we could be best friends.* Instead, Yasmine had a built-in best *enemy*.

Yago ignored his sister and kept talking to his parents. "I told Brent—my new coach—about how many goals I scored last season," he said. "I bet he starts me on the front line in our game this Saturday."

"I'm sure he will." Mr. Madrigal was beaming. "And I bet you're going to score even more goals this season. You're bigger and stronger than you were in the fall."

That's true, Yasmine thought. Yago had grown even more than she had that winter. For the first time she could remember, her brother was actually taller than she was.

Yago nodded, taking another big bite of bread. He washed it down with half a glass of milk and then turned to his mother.

"I want you to get all my goals on tape," he told Mrs. Madrigal. "Then, at the end of the season, I can make my own personal highlights tape."

Oh, please, Yasmine thought. *Who would want to watch that?*

But Mr. Madrigal was nodding. "Good idea," he said. "You could do that all through high school, and then put a highlight tape in your college applications. Maybe you'll even get a soccer scholarship that way!"

Yasmine rolled her eyes. Her dad worked at Beachside High School as a guidance counselor, helping kids decide what they wanted to do after graduation. He was always giving the twins advice on applying to college—even though they wouldn't be ready to go for another seven years! Besides, Yasmine thought her parents were paying way too much attention to Yago.

"My game is on Saturday, too," Yasmine put in.

Mrs. Madrigal nodded. "You guys are playing at the same time on side-by-side fields. Dad and I are going to have a very exciting afternoon trying to watch both games at once."

Yasmine frowned. She didn't want her parents to miss half *her* game just because they were watching Yago's.

"Please try to pay special attention when I'm playing attacker," Yasmine said. "I don't want you to miss any of the goals I make."

"Ha!" Yago said. "Don't hold your breath. Yaz never makes goals."

"For your information, I made four last spring." Yasmine gave her brother a dirty look.

"Big whoopee," Yago said. "I made at least forty."

You wish *you made forty goals,* Yasmine addressed her brother silently. The real number was closer to twenty, she knew. But it was pointless to argue with Yago.

Yasmine turned to look at her father. "Scoring goals isn't everything," she said, shooting a look at Yago. "So try not to miss any spectacular defensive plays I make, either. Unlike *some* people, I'm a terrific defender."

Mr. Madrigal sighed. "Well, I'll do my best to see all your important plays. But I have two kids and only one set of eyes. Chances are I'm going to miss something."

Yago scraped up all his peas and put the whole mess in his mouth. "Being a twin stinks," he mumbled.

Yasmine didn't say anything. But she couldn't have agreed more.

chapter 4

"HERE WE ARE—IN PLENTY OF TIME FOR the big games," Mrs. Di Gregorio said as she slowed her green station wagon to turn into the parking lot at the Beachside playing fields. Geena was thankful that her family was arriving early. She wanted some time to practice before the rest of the Stars arrived. She didn't have much time to drill while she was home—she was too busy helping her parents. As the oldest of seven kids, Geena had a lot of responsibilities. After her came Peter, ten; Marco, nine; Naomi, seven; Luca, four; Isabella, two; and baby Sophia, who was just six months old.

That afternoon, Mrs. Di Gregorio, Marco, and Sophia were coming to cheer for Geena and Peter, who had side-by-side games. Mr. Di Gregorio had taken the other three kids shoe shopping.

"Is something wrong, Geena?" Mrs. Di Gregorio asked as she pulled the car into a parking space near the field. "You've been quiet all the way over here."

Geena made a face. "I guess I'm a little nervous."

"I'm not," Peter said confidently. "I hope my coach lets me play goalkeeper."

"Yikes—I hope Marina doesn't ask *me* to be goalkeeper," Geena said anxiously. "I don't have a clue how to tend a goal."

"Don't worry!" Marco said as he flung off his seat belt. "I'm sure your team will win, Geena."

"I don't really care if we win," Geena told Marco as they climbed out of the car. "I just don't want us to lose because I make a stupid mistake."

"But your team is good, right?" Marco persisted as they waited for Mrs. Di Gregorio to unfasten Sophia's car seat.

Geena considered and then started to giggle. "Actually, I really don't know. Some of the players seem good to me, but I'm not exactly an expert."

Mrs. Di Gregorio picked up Sophia and smiled at Geena. "Just try your best and have a good time," she said.

Geena nodded. "That's what Marina says too."

The family walked over to the field, and Geena got to work practicing her dribbling. After a few minutes, Geena spotted Sarah and hurried over to join her. "So are you ready for our first game?" Geena asked.

"Absolutely," Sarah said enthusiastically. "It's going to be fun, right?"

Geena smiled back at her new friend. She was starting to relax a little as the rest of her teammates arrived at the field. "Right!"

★

"Gather round, everybody!" Marina called.

Tess and Tameka had been warming up together on the sidelines. Now they ran to meet Marina and the rest of the Stars on the aluminum bench that had been set up near the field. On the adjacent field, the Suns were meeting with their coach.

"Before I tell you your positions," Marina said, "I want to remind all of you that our league plays short-sided teams. That means that we can play only nine players at once."

Tess loved playing short-sided. Traditional soccer teams have eleven players, but short-sided teams have as few as seven. That meant that each player had more time with the coaches, more time on the field—and more time with the ball. A chance to play on a short-sided team was one of the reasons Tess had switched to the AYSO league.

"So two of us will always be sitting out?" Jordan asked.

"Right," Marina said. "But I'll make sure everyone gets to play an equal amount of time. Don't think you've done anything wrong just because I pull you out. Okay?"

The girls all nodded.

"Good," Marina said. She pulled a list out of her jeans. "Fiona, will you please play goalkeeper?"

"Sure," Fiona answered.

Marina smiled and tossed Fiona the goalkeeper's gloves and multicolored jersey. Then she glanced down at her list. "Jordan, I'd like you to play center defender. Rose, left defender. And Yaz, you'll be our right defender."

"But I wanted to play attacker," Yasmine complained.

"I didn't forget," Marina reassured her. "And I promise you'll get a chance on the front line. You just might have to wait until next week's game."

"Okay," Yasmine said. But she looked disappointed.

Tess shifted her weight impatiently. She couldn't wait to find out what position *she* was going to play. Tess let her gaze wander over the stands. Her mother had to work that afternoon, so she wasn't there. But Tess spotted Tameka's mom and waved to her.

"Amber and Nicole, I want you to work the midfield," Marina was saying.

Nicole and Amber traded high fives.

"Don't worry," Nicole told the others. "Nothing will get by us."

"Tameka, play right attacker," Marina went on. "Geena, left attacker."

Marina turned to smile at Tess. "Tess, I'd like you to play center attacker," she said. "And you'll also be our team captain for the day."

"Cool!" Tess said with a big grin. Being team captain meant that she got to represent the team during the coin toss. If she won the toss, she'd pick which goal the Stars would use. Tess wanted to win the toss—she liked the idea of beginning the season in control.

"That's it, everybody," Marina said. "Have fun out there."

The ref blew her whistle a few seconds later. "Captains on the field," she announced.

Tess jogged out to the ref. So did the team captain for the Galaxy. Tess thought she recognized the Galaxy player. She went to Beachside Middle School, like Tess.

"Ready, girls?" the ref asked.

Tess nodded.

The ref pointed to the Galaxy player. "Call it in the air," she said.

"Heads," the Galaxy player said.

Tess crossed her fingers as the coin landed.

"It's tails." The ref turned to Tess.

"We'll take that goal," she said, pointing behind her.

"All right, let's get this game started!" the ref said. Tess's team joined her on the field.

"Okay, guys," Tess told Tameka and Geena. "We've got the kickoff. Tameka, stay wide. I'll pass to you. Then Geena and I will run toward the goal and try to get open."

"Sounds good," Tameka said.

Geena nodded seriously.

The girls lined up while the ref inspected the ball. She put the ball down and stuck her whistle in her mouth. But before she could signal the start of play, a cheer erupted from the sidelines.

"Two! Four! Six! Eight! Who do we appreci-ate? Geena! Geena! Geena!"

Geena covered her eyes with her hands. But then she smiled and waved.

The ref raised her eyebrows. "Nice fan club."

"Thanks." Geena's cheeks had turned bright pink.

"Who is that?" Tameka asked.

"My little brother and sister," Geena explained.

"Cool." Tess smiled. She felt a tiny twinge of jealousy. Her mother hardly ever came to her games. But Geena had her own cheering section.

"Okay, let's get started," the ref said. She blew her whistle to signal the beginning of the game.

Tameka immediately shot forward.

Tess passed the ball to her. Then Tess dashed past a Galaxy midfielder, keeping even with the ball.

Tameka dribbled along the right touchline. When she saw that Tess was open, she passed the ball inside.

Tess let the ball pass slightly in front of her.

She kicked it with the inside of her cleat. The ball, powered with the force of Tess's running, soared into the air and flew into the corner of the goal. The goalkeeper jumped up, but she was too short to reach it.

"Goal—Stars!" the ref yelled.

"All right!" Tess screamed. She threw her arms around Tameka.

Geena jogged up to them. "Nice play," she said. "Boy, that didn't take long."

Tess grinned. "Sure didn't!"

The Stars regrouped at the halfway line.

"Good work, attackers," Marina called from where she was standing on the sidelines.

"Nice one, Tess," Amber said.

"Good assist, Tameka," Nicole put in.

Tess basked in her teammates' praise. She took a deep breath, enjoying the smell of slightly crushed hot grass. Tess felt completely happy. The soccer season was finally under way, and she'd scored the first goal in the Stars' first game.

The ref put the ball down and tooted her whistle.

A Galaxy player with a long black ponytail kicked the ball forward. With a few solid passes, the Galaxy team advanced toward the Stars' goal. But Jordan seized control of the ball when one of the Galaxy attacker's passes went slightly off target. She whomped the ball so hard that it came down in Galaxy territory.

Tameka and Tess dashed up the field at a dead run. Geena trailed behind, trying to keep her eye on the ball.

One of the Galaxy defenders got control of the ball. But Tess charged her and stole the ball right out from between her feet.

Like taking candy from a baby, Tess told herself as she dribbled forward. She zigzagged around a slightly more alert Galaxy defender and then looked to her left. She couldn't see Geena. She looked to her right—and there was Tameka, just where she should be, and wide open.

"Coming at you!" Tess called as she fired the ball in Tameka's direction.

Tameka connected with the ball and aimed a highly angled shot on the goal.

Tough shot, Tess thought. But to her amazement, the ball caught the inside left goalpost and bounced in.

The ref signaled again and shouted, "Goal—Stars!"

Tameka threw a fist into the air. "Yes!" she said.

Tess gave her friend an excited pat on the back. "Way to be there," she said.

"Nice pass," Tameka countered.

Geena fell into step with Tameka and Tess as they headed back to the halfway line. "You guys are really good," she said.

Tess beamed. She was ready for more. But before the girls could line up for another kickoff, the ref signaled the substitution break.

Tess shot Tameka a surprised look. "I can't believe the game is a fourth over already," she said as they jogged over to the sidelines.

"Great start," Marina said as the girls joined her. "Tess, Tameka, Jordan, you all had nice plays."

"Thanks," Tess said. She expected the coach to say something more. Something specific about her goal. And something about her assist.

But Marina hurried on. "I could see that the rest of you were really hustling. Now we don't have much time. Sarah, I want you to go in as center attacker. And Lacey, you can play right attacker."

Center attacker? Tess thought. *But that's my position!*

"Get a fast sip of water if you need it, and then hit the field," Marina said.

"Are you taking me out?" Tess asked the coach.

Marina nodded absently. Her eyes were on the field. Apparently she was watching to make sure that the team got into the right positions.

Tess felt as if someone had kicked her in the stomach. How could Marina take her out *now*? When she was on a *roll*? She took Tameka's arm and pulled her a few feet away from the coach.

"Can you believe Marina took us out?" Tess asked in a low voice. "Is she crazy, or what?"

Tameka shrugged. "Well, Lacey and Sarah haven't played yet. And besides . . ." Tameka let her voice trail off. She was following the action on the field.

"Besides *what*?" Tess demanded.

Tameka looked a little embarrassed. "Well, we scored twice in the first quarter. Maybe we were playing a little *too* well. I mean, maybe Marina wanted to give the Galaxy players a chance to score."

Tess couldn't believe what she was hearing.

Playing *too* well? Sometimes Tameka took this nice-girl thing to an extreme.

"Ouch!" Tameka suddenly exclaimed.

"What?" Tess spun around to face the field. "Did someone score?"

"No," Tameka said. "Sarah tripped over the ball. I hope she's okay."

"Maybe she'll have to come out," Tess said hopefully. But Sarah was already back on her feet.

Tess sighed and flopped down in the grass to watch the game.

About five minutes into the quarter, Lacey missed a pass because she was busy waving at Yasmine's brother, Yago.

"What's he doing over here?" Tess grumbled. "I thought the Suns were playing on the other field."

"He's getting a drink from his mom," Tameka said.

"And distracting our players," Tess grumped.

Tameka laughed. "You have to admit, he *is* cute."

"Well, yeah," Tess agreed. "But Lacey should pay attention to the game!"

Before halftime, the Galaxy had scored not one, not two, but *three* goals. Tess's good mood disappeared along with the Stars' lead.

chapter 5

"I CAN'T BELIEVE WE LOST OUR LEAD," Tess said during halftime.

A couple of the nearby Stars glanced up at Tess. But then they turned their attention back to the five-gallon water cooler Amber and her parents had brought. The afternoon was warm and sticky, and everyone wanted a drink.

Tameka gave her friend a sympathetic smile. "Don't worry," she said. "We'll catch up during the second half. Right, everybody?"

"Sure," Amber said with a shrug. She held a bag of orange slices out to Tess. "These oranges were grown without the use of pesticides," she announced proudly.

Tess accepted a slice. She didn't really feel like eating. But she knew the natural sugar in the orange would help keep up her energy in the second half.

Sarah smiled at Amber and pulled several orange slices out of the bag. She wiped her arm across her forehead. "I was super-glad when the ref blew her whistle. I don't think I could've run down the field one more time without collapsing."

"Maybe you should sit out the next quarter," Tess said hopefully. "We wouldn't want you to have a heart attack or anything."

"Nah," Sarah said. "I feel better now."

Amber winked at her. "Must be these organic oranges."

Tess got to her feet. Marina was walking over and Tess wanted her to see that she was ready to get back in the game. She listened eagerly as the coach began to speak.

"Today is the first time I've seen you playing together as a team," Marina said. "And I've noticed lots of good work. But I also see some things we can improve. Once or twice, a few of you chased after the ball at the same time. Try not to bunch up like that. Remember, it's important for the person with the ball to have someone to pass to."

Tess nodded. Marina's point was important. Good soccer players were always sensitive to their teammates' positions on the field. Tess looked at Sarah, who'd spent most of the second quarter on Geena's heels whenever Geena had the ball.

But Sarah didn't seem to be paying any attention to the coach. She was reaching for the bag of orange slices and humming softly to herself. She didn't even notice that she had knocked over Geena's cup of water.

Tess felt a flash of frustration. Sarah wouldn't improve if she didn't even realize she was doing anything wrong.

Marina started to go through the lineup. Tess was relieved when Marina kept her promise and put her and Tameka back in. "Tess, I'd like you in front center," the coach said. "Tameka, will you play left attacker this time?"

"Sure," Tameka agreed.

"Lacey, stay in as right attacker," Marina said. "Nicole and Amber, stay in the midfield."

Tess smiled with satisfaction. So far, the lineup sounded great. They had a strong attacking line and midfield—perfect for tying up the score.

"Jordan and Yaz, I'd like you to hang out on the

sidelines with me for a while," Marina continued. "Rose, stay in as left defender. Sarah, play center defender. Geena, right defender. Fiona, stay in as goalkeeper. Have a great half, guys!"

As the girls walked onto the field, Tess caught Fiona's eye.

"Marina put all the beginners on defense," Tess commented.

Fiona made a face. "It's a goalkeeper's nightmare. I mean, I like Sarah and Rose and Geena. But none of them really know what they're doing."

"Don't worry," Tess said. "The ball is going to spend the entire half in Galaxy territory."

"Sounds good to me," Fiona said with a grin.

Tess jogged up to the halfway line. She motioned for Tameka and Lacey to come closer.

"Listen," Tess whispered urgently to the other attackers. "Our defense is a little weak. We've got to help Fiona."

Lacey raised her bushy eyebrows. "We're attackers. How can we help the goalkeeper?"

"By keeping the ball in Galaxy territory," Tess said.

"No problem." Tameka clapped her hands. "Let's go."

But Tess didn't look away from Lacey's hazel eyes. "We're going to have to concentrate to keep the ball away from our goal. That means no flirting while the ball is in play."

Lacey grinned. "What fun is soccer if you can't flirt during the game?"

Tess groaned.

"I'm just kidding," Lacey said, shaking her head. "I promise to pay attention."

"Thanks," Tess said with relief.

The Galaxy center passed the ball to her left, where one of her teammates was waiting. The girl got control of the ball and started to drive it up the left touchline. But Lacey raced after her, batting at the ball with her feet.

After several yards, the Galaxy player got aggravated. She passed the ball into the center of the field.

The Galaxy center sprinted forward. But Nicole got there first. Since the Galaxy center was bearing down on her, she immediately passed the ball forward to Tess.

Tess turned to face the ball, which hit her square in the chest. She pulled her rib cage back, and the ball dropped to her feet. Tess only had a chance to dribble a few feet when two Galaxy midfielders rushed up to challenge her.

Where's Tameka? Tess wondered. She glanced off to her left. But a Galaxy player was covering Tameka.

"I'm open!"

Tess recognized Lacey's voice. But she couldn't see her teammate. All Tess could see was a blur of blue as the Galaxy players moved in even closer. So she pretended she was going to pass left. When the Galaxy players followed the motion of her feet, Tess passed right—in the direction of Lacey's voice.

Too late, the Galaxy players realized what had happened, and dashed off after Lacey and the ball. Tess found herself open again.

I guess we're not the only team that's having trouble bunching up, Tess thought as she sprinted toward the goal.

Tess chased the pack downfield. She couldn't see the ball because the group of Galaxy players was in the way. But they fanned out just in time for Tess to see Lacey shoot straight into the goal. That tied up the score.

Cheers exploded from the smattering of parents sitting behind the touchline. Marina was shaking one fist in the air, and Mr. Thomas was grinning broadly.

"All right!" Tess shouted. She jogged over to Lacey and patted her on her back. "Way to go!"

Lacey was leaning forward, hands on her knees, fighting for breath. But she was also smiling. "Thanks!"

On the next play, the Stars weren't so lucky. This time a Galaxy attacker faked Lacey out. She advanced the ball several yards, then sent a long bouncing pass diagonally across the field. Nicole and Amber both reacted too slowly to stop it. But a Galaxy player was waiting. She practically pounced on the ball.

Tess's heart sank when she realized that only Rose and Fiona were between the Galaxy player and the goal. *So much for keeping the ball in Galaxy territory,* she thought.

The Galaxy's right attacker drove forward.

Tess took a closer look at Rose, who seemed to be in another world with a dreamy look on her face. *What is she thinking about?* Tess wondered. Rose didn't even seem to realize the ball was nearby.

"Hey, Rose!" Tess hollered. "Get in her way."

Marina, Fiona, and the other players were calling to Rose too. Eventually the redhead snapped out of her daydream and realized she needed to do something. But by then, the Galaxy player had already passed her.

Fiona was ready. She stood just inside the goal, legs spread wide. She held her arms out to the side, ready to pounce.

The Galaxy player drew back her leg and kicked the ball with all her might. The ball arced high in the air, heading into the hardest-to-reach spot at the top corner of the goal.

Fiona sprang up. She seemed only to graze the ball with her fingertips as she flew through the air. But that slight touch was enough to change the ball's direction, and it came down outside the goal.

"Kick it!" Fiona called to Geena as she landed on her side.

Geena looked terrified. But she got behind the ball and kicked it forward to Nicole.

Tess, who was bug-eyed from Fiona's amazing save, realized it was time for her to get into position. "Way to go, Fiona. Geena, you too!"

The rest of the quarter passed swiftly. Tess and

Tameka each made another drive toward the goal, although neither one scored. At the substitution break, the game was still tied.

"Good work," Marina told the girls as they came off the field and got a quick sip of water.

Tess stood up a little straighter. *It was a great quarter,* she thought.

"We don't have much time," Marina said. "So listen up for the substitutions. Jordan, go in for Geena. And Yaz, go in for Tess."

Tess couldn't believe her ears. As the other girls took the field, she stood staring at Marina. She was unhappy that Marina had taken her out. But that wasn't what was bothering her the most.

"What's the matter?" Marina asked.

"I—I don't understand why you're putting Yaz in as an attacker," Tess blurted out. "She's much better at defense."

"I know," Marina said. "But she wants to get better at scoring. And she can't do that without practice."

Tess fought an urge to stomp her foot. "Couldn't she practice during *practice*?" she demanded. "The score is tied!"

Marina turned away from the field and gave

her full attention to Tess. "I know winning is important to you," she said, her brown eyes serious. "But I think it's more important that everyone get an equal chance to play. That way, when we do win, we'll all get to celebrate together."

Tess saw Geena staring at her, and she realized that she had been shouting. Taking a deep breath, Tess walked off down the sidelines. She struggled to get her emotions under control. Maybe she was taking the game too seriously.

Just then, the handful of spectators groaned. Tess turned to the field in time to see a Galaxy player shoot on the goal.

The ball soared over Fiona's head—and in.

"What happened?" Tess called to Geena.

Geena shook her head. But she looked amused. "Sarah passed the ball right to a Galaxy player," she reported. "She must feel awful."

"Oh no," Tess mumbled under her breath. Just like that, the tie that she'd worked so hard to achieve disappeared.

And it stayed disappeared.

When the ref blew her whistle to signal the end of the game, the score was Galaxy 4, Stars 3.

chapter 6

"ORDER WHATEVER YOU WANT," MARINA told the Stars at the ice cream parlor after the game. "Just no banana splits, okay?"

Yasmine looked at the blackboard over the counter that listed all the flavors, and tried to decide what to order. Usually she loved the ice cream at Tosca's. But nothing sounded good today. Yasmine really wasn't in the mood for ice cream.

"What are you going to get?" she asked Lacey, who was standing in front of her in line.

"Peppermint cone," Lacey replied. "And a big glass of water. I'm really thirsty."

"It's all that running around," Yasmine said. *Running around—that's about all you did in the fourth quarter,* she reminded herself. During the game, Yasmine had been really excited when Marina put her in the front line. But now she had to admit that she had blown her chance to show everyone what a great attacker she could be. Had she even come close to scoring a goal in those entire twelve and a half minutes? No.

"Running around—and drooling," Nicole, who was standing behind Yasmine, added. "I swear, Lacey, the minute a cute boy appears, you start panting."

"Speaking of cute . . ." Lacey ignored Nicole and turned to address Yasmine. "Your brother is very good-looking."

"Yago?" Yasmine made a sour face. "Yuck!"

"Shhh," Lacey said. "I don't want him to hear us."

All of the boys on the Sun team were sitting together at a table near the windows, with their coach.

Yasmine didn't want Yago to overhear what Lacey was saying, either. Her brother was already stuck on himself. She didn't want him to get even worse.

The girls had gotten to the front of the line.

"May I help you?" asked the pimply teenager behind the counter.

"Vanilla cone," Yasmine said. *A perfectly boring order for a completely no-talent player,* she told herself.

Yasmine waited while Nicole and Lacey collected their ice cream. Then she walked with them to join the rest of the Stars at a long table against the wall.

Tess and Tameka were sitting at one end of the table. They were whispering together about something. *What's up with them?* Yasmine wondered.

She couldn't really find out because Marina, Amber, and Jordan had already filled the seats on that half of the table.

Fiona, Geena, Rose, and Sarah were sitting together near the other end of the table. Sarah had already finished most of a hot fudge sundae. A glob of fudge was hanging from her bangs.

"One of the Galaxy players looked just like you," Sarah was telling Geena as Yasmine slid into a seat. "That's why I passed her the ball. I thought she was you!"

"Is that what happened?" Fiona asked. "I thought your pass just didn't go where you wanted it to."

"No, it was right on target." Sarah laughed. "Right on the *wrong* target."

"Next time, try looking for a yellow jersey instead of a familiar face," Yasmine suggested.

Sarah giggled. "Good idea," she mumbled with her mouth full.

"Don't you feel bad about blowing the play—and the game?" Geena asked.

"Nah," Sarah said, digging her spoon into the sundae. "I mean, I've only been playing soccer for a few weeks. I don't expect to be perfect yet."

Suddenly Sarah's eyes widened. "You don't think . . . Is the rest of the team mad at me for messing up?" she asked, as if the thought was a new one.

Nicole shot a glance toward Tess at the other end of the table. "Don't worry about it," she told Sarah.

"I made some stupid mistakes too," Rose said reassuringly.

"I'm not mad at you," Yasmine said honestly. "The only person I'm mad at is me. I can't believe I didn't score."

"You played a good game," Fiona said.

"Not as good as you," Yasmine said. "If we'd

chosen a most valuable player for the game, you definitely would have been in the running. That save was beautiful!"

Fiona looked a little self-conscious as a smile of satisfaction spread over her face. "Thanks! You know, I hardly ever played goalkeeper last season. But I think I might be good at it."

"You definitely are," Yasmine said. She took a big lick of her ice cream, which was starting to melt over her hand. She was beginning to feel a little better. *Maybe I'm being too hard on myself,* she thought. *After all, one measly quarter isn't that much time to score.*

But Yasmine's mood took a dive when she saw Yago heading toward her table. The rest of the Suns were moving toward the door.

"What do you want?" Yasmine grumbled at her brother.

Lacey kicked her under the table. *Be nice,* she mouthed silently.

"Mom's coming to pick us up," Yago told Yasmine. "She'll be here in ten minutes."

"Why don't you sit down, Yago?" Lacey said.

To Yasmine's amazement, Yago smiled and then

slumped into the only empty seat at the table—right next to Sarah.

Sarah's eyes lit up, and she gave Yago a big grin. *It looks like Lacey isn't the only boy-crazy Star,* Yasmine thought. She couldn't get over the fact that her friends thought Yago was cute. How totally creepy!

"How was your game?" Yago asked.

"Great," Lacey said. "How was *yours?*"

"Very great," Yago said with a grin. "I scored two goals."

Yasmine almost dropped what was left of her ice cream cone. "Two?" she repeated.

"Yup," Yago said. "How many did you make?"

"None." Yasmine could barely speak.

Yago smiled gleefully—just as Yasmine knew he would.

"Looks like I'm still the family high scorer," Yago said with a smirk. "Always have been, always will be."

"We've only played one game," Yasmine defended herself. "I played front line for exactly twelve and a half minutes. Just wait—I'm going to start putting them in."

"Yeah," Nicole said. "I bet Yaz scores more goals than you do by the end of the season."

Yasmine shot Nicole a warning look. She wasn't at all sure she could make more goals than Yago. After all, Yago had been playing attacker for years, and Yasmine was just learning the position.

Yago was laughing. "I wouldn't bet on that," he said. "In fact, I wouldn't even bet that Yasmine will make one goal the entire season."

"But I made four last season!" Yasmine exclaimed.

"Luck," Yago said with a grin.

Yasmine felt her hand clench. Why did Yago always have to be so insulting?

"If you're so sure I won't score, why don't we bet on it?" Yasmine demanded.

Yago's smile faded slightly. But he held out his hand. "Deal," he said.

Yasmine shook his hand. "Deal."

★

"Tess! Tameka!"

It was just before soccer practice on Tuesday afternoon, and Tess and Tameka were walking to the field together. Mr. Thomas was in Chicago on business, so he was missing practice that afternoon.

Tess shielded her eyes from the sun and peered up at the Madrigals' neat frame house. Yasmine was waving at them from the porch.

"Wait up!" Yasmine called. Letting the screen door bang, she dashed down the walk in front of her house and joined Tess and Tameka on the sidewalk.

Just up ahead, Yago was walking in the same direction.

"Where's your brother going?" Tess asked.

"Soccer practice," Yago said.

"Should we walk with him?" Tameka asked.

Yasmine made a face. "No way. I'm avoiding him."

Tess and Tameka exchanged looks. Yasmine always seemed to be fighting with her twin brother.

"Ever since Saturday, he's been bragging about how he made two goals last weekend—and I didn't make any," Yasmine explained. "If I have to listen to him for another minute, I'm going to scream."

Tameka gave Yasmine a sympathetic look. "That sounds rough."

"It is," Yasmine agreed. "And the worst part is that my dad actually encourages him! Ever since last Saturday, Dad's been calling Yago 'the family high scorer.' I've *got* to score in the next game. If I don't, I'll never shut Yago up."

When the girls turned into the field, Nicole waved and came over to say hello. While the other girls chatted, Tess considered Yasmine's problem. She waited until there was a break in the conversation, and then she got Yasmine's attention.

"If you really want to be a good attacker," Tess told Yasmine, "you need to learn how to read the field and control the ball—"

"Speaking of controlling the ball, check out Sarah," Nicole interrupted.

The tall girl was already on the field. She was trying to juggle a ball on her thighs. But the ball kept flying out of control.

Watching Sarah's clumsy attempts made Tess feel a little depressed. With players like that, the Stars would never win games.

"Forget about reading the field," Nicole said. "If you really want to score, you should figure out a way to get rid of players like Sarah."

"Nicole!" Tameka looked shocked. "Sarah's a member of our team. You shouldn't talk about her that way!"

Nicole patted Tameka on the back. "Don't freak out," she said with a laugh. "I'm just kidding. Come on, let's go warm up."

Tameka, Nicole, and Yasmine trotted off to join Sarah.

But Tess hesitated for a moment before following them. The conversation had given her an idea.

The Stars aren't going to lose any more games, Tess told herself. *Not if I can help it.*

"LET'S GET STARTED!" MARINA CALLED ON Thursday afternoon at the beginning of practice.

Tess quickly put the ball that she and Tameka had been playing with back into its net bag. She was eager for practice to start. The Stars' second game was only two days away, and Tess wanted to be ready.

Marina was staring at Lacey and Sarah, who were sitting under the big oak tree at the end of the field, deep in conversation. They didn't seem to notice that practice was about to begin.

"Do you want me to go get them?" Tess offered.

Marina nodded. "Thanks, Tess."

"No prob," Tess said. She ran toward the end of the field.

"So what did you tell him?" Lacey was asking as Tess approached.

"I told him no," Sarah replied. "I mean, he's really cute and everything. But the play is next Saturday at two o'clock."

"What are you guys talking about?" Tess asked.

"Sarah just got asked on her first date!" Lacey's eyes were shining.

That was *interesting news,* Tess thought. Tess wasn't as boy-crazy as Lacey was. But she definitely wouldn't mind if some cute guy asked her out.

"Where are you going?" Tess asked.

"Nowhere," Sarah said, looking disappointed. "Jeff asked me to a play with his family. But it starts at exactly the same time as our game."

"I'd never miss a game for a date," Tess said.

Lacey was looking at Tess like she was nuts. "Well, *I* would never miss a date for a game," she told Sarah. The minute the words were out of Lacey's mouth, Tess had an idea. Here was the perfect chance to put her plan in action.

Tess shrugged as casually as she could. "I guess

that just goes to show, two people can see the same situation completely differently. Sarah, you really should decide what's right for you."

Sarah thought for a moment. "I want to come to the game."

Wrong answer! Tess thought unhappily.

"Maybe Jeff could come watch us," Lacey said.

"No chance," Sarah said. "His sister is in the play. And he promised her he'd be there."

"Do you think he'll invite someone else to go with him?" Tess asked, thinking fast.

"Probably," Sarah said as she got to her feet.

Lacey's bushy eyebrows shot up. "Another *girl*?"

Sarah shrugged. "Maybe."

"Gee," Tess said. "Wouldn't it be awful if you and Jeff were soul mates? I mean, if destiny meant for you to spend the rest of your lives together—"

Sarah giggled. "That doesn't sound awful!"

"What would be awful," Tess explained, "is if Jeff fell in love with the girl he takes to the play in your place."

Lacey's eyes widened. "Without your soul mate, you'd have to spend the rest of your life alone!"

Excuse me while I barf, Tess thought. But she forced herself to keep a serious expression.

Sarah was biting her lip. "So you guys think I should go?"

"It's up to you," Tess said solemnly.

"Think about it," Lacey suggested.

"I will," Sarah said with a worried look.

Tess was pretty sure Sarah would pick Jeff over soccer. *One down. Two to go.*

Hmmm, Geena thought as she ran her finger down the row of books. *I wonder if the library has gotten any new young adult titles.*

Friday afternoon was Geena's favorite time of the week. That was when her mother took the entire family to the Beachside Public Library to pick out books.

Geena loved coming to the little library, with its low round tables and colorful posters.

The only problem was that over the past few years, she had worked her way through most of the young adult titles the library owned. *Today must be my lucky day,* Geena thought. She quickly found a book she'd never read. After glancing around to make sure that Naomi and Marco weren't getting into any trouble, she headed over to the magazine rack and pulled out the latest issue of *Fourteen* magazine.

Geena adored *Fourteen*. She'd tried to get her mother to order her a subscription, but Mrs. Di Gregorio had said it was a waste of money. Geena knew that if she wanted the magazine, she'd have to save up to buy it herself. So far she hadn't been able to do that, so she read as much as possible at the library.

Wow, what a great outfit, Geena thought as she studied the cover model. *I wish I could wear clothes like that to school instead of my stupid uniform.*

Geena took the magazine over to the comfortable couches. She did a double take as she passed the tables near the encyclopedias. *Could it be?*

"Tess?" Geena asked. "Tess—what are you doing here?"

Tess looked surprised to see Geena as she glanced up from a stack of books. "Hi! I'm working on a report for school. I'm writing about the new pro women's soccer league."

"Really? What class is that for?"

"English. It's extra credit, so we get to choose our own topics."

Geena's eyebrows flew up. *Extra credit?* Tess totally didn't seem like the type.

"Don't look so shocked," Tess said with a laugh. "I'm a total nerd. I always get straight As. And I even joined the chess club this year."

"Oh." Geena couldn't think of what else to say. Tess was so into soccer that she had a hard time imagining her life off the field.

"What are you reading?" Tess asked.

"The best magazine in the whole world," Geena told her.

"Fourteen?" Tess asked.

"Of course!" Geena said. "What else?"

"One of my relatives works at *Fourteen*," Tess said. "My aunt Sally."

"Really?" Geena was excited. Tess knew an actual person who worked at *Fourteen*. "That is so awesome! I'd love to have a job like that someday."

"Me too." Tess's face suddenly flushed. "Especially since . . . well, nothing." She looked back down at her books.

Geena felt her fingers start to tingle. She could

tell Tess knew something about *Fourteen*. Something big.

"You know a secret." Geena leaned closer to Tess. "Please tell me."

"Well . . ." Tess didn't seem anxious to tell Geena.

"I promise I won't tell anyone," Geena said.

"Okay. . . ." Tess glanced down at her lap and bit her lip. "Um—*Fourteen* is doing a story about soccer. My aunt is in charge of picking a girl to be on the magazine's cover—"

"A model," Geena supplied.

"Right," Tess said. "Except they don't want a professional model. Their idea is to get a girl who really plays soccer."

Geena considered. "I think that's a great idea. That way the cover shot will look more realistic."

"That's exactly what Aunt Sally thought, too." Tess blinked. She seemed to be looking at something over Geena's shoulder. "But she didn't know where to find a girl. So I suggested that she come to our game on Saturday and pick someone there."

"That's amazing!" Geena gasped. "Do you think I can meet her?"

Tess finally met Geena's gaze. "Would you want to be on the cover?"

Geena laughed so loudly that the librarian gave her a dirty look. "I'm sure your aunt will pick you," she said in a low tone.

"Oh, she can't," Tess said. "That's against the rules."

"She still won't pick me," Geena said with certainty. "Models are graceful and I'm a total klutz."

Tess shook her head. "Sarah is a total klutz. You're not that bad. Besides, models are supposed to be tall, and you're one of the tallest Stars."

"But," Geena argued, "your aunt will want a good player. And I'm practically the worst Star there is."

"That's true," Tess admitted. "But my aunt doesn't have to know that. You could make up some excuse and sit out Saturday's game. I'd tell Aunt Sally you're a really strong player."

"You'd help me trick your aunt?" Geena was shocked. She would *never* help anyone lie to her family. But she didn't tell Tess that. After all, she didn't want Tess to change her mind.

"Anything for a teammate," Tess said.

"Thanks so much!" Geena exclaimed.

"You're welcome." Tess looked almost embarrassed.

Geena shivered as she looked down at the magazine cover. *That could be me someday soon,* she thought. It was almost too good to be true. Geena congratulated herself again for joining the Stars. Not only had she met new people, she'd met new people who knew people who worked at *Fourteen.*

Tess let out her breath as she watched Geena walk away. A feeling of relief—and amazement—spread through her stomach. *I can't believe I ran into Geena and came up with that nutty story,* Tess thought. *Fooling people is much easier than I ever imagined.*

Two down. One to go.

chapter 8

"HELLO?" TESS SAID ON FRIDAY AFTERNOON.

"Hi, this is Tess's soccer coach calling." Marina's voice sounded a bit breathless.

"Hi, Marina. This is Tess. What's up?"

"The time for our game on Saturday has been changed," Marina said in a rush. "I think there was some scheduling problem with the refs. Instead of two o'clock, we're playing at one."

"No problem," Tess said. She scribbled a note on the pad her mother kept by the phone.

"I'm glad I caught you," Marina said. "I have three classes at the university this afternoon. And now I have all these phone calls to make. . . ."

"Why don't I call Tameka for you?" Tess offered.

"That would be great," Marina said. She still sounded a little frazzled.

"Do you want me to call anybody else?" Tess asked. "I'm not doing anything important."

"Would you?" Marina sounded relieved. "Thanks, Tess, that would be a big help. Besides Tameka, why don't you call Amber, Lacey, and Rose?"

"No problem," Tess said. She jotted down the names on the pad next to where she had written "one o'clock."

"Do you have the numbers?" Marina asked.

"Yup," Tess said. "They're right here on my game schedule." Tess's mother had attached the blue sheet to the refrigerator with a magnet.

"Thanks again," Marina said. "You're an angel."

Tess made the first three calls quickly. Tameka, Amber, and Lacey were all out, so Tess left messages with their parents. She was halfway through dialing Rose's number when an idea hit her.

Tess quickly hung up the phone and wiped her sweaty palms on her jeans. *Do it,* she told herself.

Before she could have second thoughts, she picked up the phone and dialed.

The phone rang once. Twice. And then someone scooped it off the hook. "O'Connor residence," came a crisp adult voice.

Tess cleared her throat. "May I speak to Rose, please?" she said, trying not to sound as guilty as she felt.

"Who's calling?"

"Tess Adams, from her soccer team."

"Just a minute."

Tess waited for Rose to come to the phone, her heart hammering. *Maybe I should just hang up,* Tess thought. But then she remembered that she'd already given her name.

"Hello?" Over the phone, Rose sounded about six years old.

"Um—hi, Rose. It's Tess."

"Tess! Hi, what's up?"

"Um, Marina asked me to give you a call. The time for our game on Saturday has been changed. It's going to start at three o'clock now."

"Oh," Rose said. "Just a minute . . ."

Tess heard a lot of noise on the other end of

the phone. It sounded as if Rose was pawing through a pile of papers and knocking half of them to the ground.

"Saturday at three," Rose said. "I'm writing that down to be sure I don't forget. I wouldn't want to miss the game, right?"

"Right," Tess echoed.

"Okay—see you then," Rose said cheerfully.

Tess swallowed the lump that was forming in her throat. "See you then," she said as she hung up. She couldn't believe how easy it had been to tell Rose the wrong game time.

Three down, none to go, Tess thought. Her plan was working perfectly. She just wished she didn't feel so guilty about it.

★

"Hat-hat-choo!"

"God bless you," Geena said.

"Thunks," Fiona said. "Sprigg is a tough tibe for allergies."

The girls had just arrived at the playing field for Saturday's game. Geena watched as her teammate pulled a tissue out of her shorts and soundly blew her nose.

Poor Fiona, Geena thought. *She really looks mis-*

erable. Geena admired the way her teammate never complained about her asthma or allergies. *If I felt as bad as Fiona looks, I'd probably never get out of bed,* Geena thought.

Fiona rubbed her fingertips over her red-rimmed eyes. Then her eyes widened. "Wow, Geena!" she said. "You look great."

Geena felt her face get hot. But she was pleased that Fiona noticed all the hard work she'd put into her hair and makeup. Maybe Tess's aunt would notice too. And then Geena would be on her way to fame and fortune as a *Fourteen* cover model.

"Thanks," Geena said modestly.

"You really look super," Fiona said. "But if your hair is like mine, it won't stay curled long, once you start running around on the field."

That's why I'm not going to run around on the field, Geena told herself.

"Why are you wearing makeup and everything to a soccer game?" Fiona asked.

Geena had guessed her teammates would ask her that question, so she had come prepared.

"My family went out to a restaurant for lunch today," Geena told Fiona. "It's my cousin's birthday."

What Geena said was true, in a way. Her family *was* celebrating her cousin's birthday that afternoon. But that wasn't the real reason Geena was dressed up.

"I love birthdays," Fiona said. "Did your cousin have a good party?"

"The best." Geena wrapped her arms around her stomach. "The only problem is that I think I ate too much."

Geena felt bad lying to her teammate. But she told herself it was for a good cause.

About five minutes before game time, the rest of the Stars gathered under the big oak tree as Marina announced the lineup.

"We're a little shorthanded today," Marina announced. She gave Geena a sympathetic look. "Geena isn't feeling well."

"Sorry, guys," Geena said with a frown.

What should I tell Geena when she realizes that my aunt Sally isn't going to show up? Tess wondered. But then she forced herself to push that worry out of her mind. *I'll just say Aunt Sally got stuck in traffic.*

"And Sarah called to tell me she had an important appointment today," Marina went on.

Lacey caught Tess's eye. They both broke into grins.

"I hope Sarah is having a fun time with Jeff," Tess whispered to Lacey.

Marina glanced down at her list. "Does anybody know what happened to Rose?" she asked.

Tess felt a guilty twinge in her stomach, but she didn't say anything.

"Maybe she's sick," Tameka suggested.

"She probably just forgot," Jordan said. "She missed school once because she thought it was Sunday."

Marina turned to Tess. "Did you remember to call Rose?"

"Yes," Tess whispered. *That's not really a lie,* she comforted herself. *I did call her.*

"Well, I guess something must have come up," Marina said with a sigh. "And it's bad timing, too. I wanted Rose to be captain for the day."

Suddenly Tess felt terribly guilty about telling Rose the wrong time. Rose would have loved being captain. But then Tess reminded herself that the captain for the day always also played center attacker. *Not a good position for Rose,* Tess thought. *With her as center attacker, we'd never score.*

"I want you girls to call me or Mr. Thomas if you have to miss a game," Marina was saying. "But you should try *not* to miss any. Remember, you made a commitment when you joined the team. Your teammates are counting on you."

Tess just didn't understand why Marina was making such a fuss about Rose missing the game. It wasn't as if they'd *lose* because Rose wasn't there.

MARINA PUT TESS IN AS RIGHT MID-
fielder. *I guess midfield isn't that bad,* Tess thought.
*At least I'm still within striking distance of the
goal.* The game started, and as she concentrated
on the action at the front line, Tess noticed a
trouble spot.

"Be careful, Jordan," Tess called. "The Asteroids are all over you. Tameka's open!"

Jordan took Tess's advice and passed. Tameka
quickly started driving into Asteroid territory.
Tess ran forward, trying to stay open in case the
front line needed to pass back to her. But the Asteroids' defense couldn't stop the Stars' drive.
Tameka got deep into Asteroid territory before

one of the Asteroids challenged her and kicked the ball out.

Tameka took the throw-in. Since the same alert Asteroid had glued herself to Lacey, Tameka threw the ball to Yasmine.

The throw was long, and Yasmine had to chase the ball into the corner of the field. By the time she managed to turn it around, two Asteroid defenders had descended on her. One stood between her and the goalkeeper, and the other aggressively tried to steal the ball from her.

"I'm open!" Tess yelled.

Yasmine heard her—and quickly passed the ball back to Tess.

Waiting until she had drawn off the Asteroid who was covering Tameka, Tess passed the ball forward to her friend.

Tameka landed a powerful left-footed kick— and the ball hit the inside of the net before the Asteroid goalkeeper had a chance to react.

A cheer erupted from the parents who had set up their chairs along the sidelines.

"Way to go, you guys," Tess told Yasmine and Lacey as the girls headed back into position.

Tameka gave Tess a high five. "Thanks," she said.

"The next goal is mine," Yasmine said.

"Go for it, girl!" Tameka encouraged her.

When play resumed, Jordan immediately drove the ball past the Asteroids' front line. But as she closed in on the goal, one of the big Asteroid defenders—number eight, Tess noticed—stole the ball and booted it to midfield.

Tess and the rest of the Stars' attacking line dashed back to the center. By then, Nicole had control of the ball. She passed it forward to Lacey.

"Watch out for number eight," Tess called as the Stars began another attack on the Asteroids' goal. Despite the warning, the same defender booted the ball back into Star territory.

Fifty seconds later the ref signaled the first substitution break. "Take two!" she announced.

Yes, Tess thought. Her yellow Stars jersey was sticking to her back. Sweat was dripping off her nose, and the strands of hair that had come out of her ponytail were soaked.

As the team came off the field, Mr. Thomas handed each girl a cup of cold water.

Tess downed hers in one gulp.

"You guys look tired," Marina said, watching them with a frown.

"We must have run back and forth a hundred times," Yasmine said.

"A hundred and *one*," Fiona said. "I was counting.

Marina shook her head. "I wish I could give a couple of you guys a rest. But I don't have any substitutes."

"Aren't you feeling any better?" Jordan asked Geena in her soft voice.

Geena, who was sitting in a chair under the oak tree, gave Tess a questioning look.

Tess shrugged—as if to say *I don't know where Aunt Sally is, but she could be here any minute.*

"My stomach still hurts," Geena said.

"That's okay," Tess said quickly. "We don't mind playing the whole game. Right, Tameka?"

"I don't mind right now," Tameka said, crumpling up her cup. "But the game is only a quarter over."

The second quarter began with Yasmine quickly driving the ball into Asteroid territory and shooting on the goal. The shot went wide. But

Tameka managed to pounce on the ball before any of the Asteroids could, and tap it in.

Ahead by two goals, Tess thought as she trotted back into position. *Not bad.* She was happy that Tameka was having such a good game. But watching Tameka make goals wasn't nearly as much fun as making goals herself. *I'll get the next one,* Tess promised herself.

Near the end of the first half, the Asteroids' right attacker faked her way past Tameka. She dribbled the ball down the center of the field, taking it deep into Star territory.

The Star defenders—Nicole and Fiona—went to work for the first time during the game. Nicole charged the Asteroid player. The two of them battled over the ball. Tess heard a pounding noise as the girls' feet crashed into the ball over and over.

"Get it! Get it!" Tess hollered.

Both girls attacked the ball at once, but it never moved more than a few inches in any direction. Finally the Asteroid took a quick step back and gave Nicole the opening she needed to kick the ball forward a few feet and get her body between the Asteroid and the ball. Then she walloped the ball back toward the front line.

"That's the way to fight!" Marina yelled.

Tess wanted to congratulate Nicole too. But she needed all her breath to run after the ball. Tess was just crossing the halfway line when the ref signaled the end of the half.

"Great half, girls!" Mr. Thomas said as the Stars came off the field.

"Really great," Geena put in.

Tameka drank her cup of water, then lay down on the grass. "Wake me up when halftime is over," she said. "I'm wiped out."

Tess frowned at Tameka. She wished her friend wouldn't make such a big deal out of how tired she was—it made Tess feel guilty.

Yasmine lay down, and rested her head on Tameka's stomach. Now both of them were making Tess feel guilty.

Tess was hoping Marina would move her up to the front line during the second half. But the only change the coach made was to have Tameka and Nicole switch places. Now Tameka was playing left defender, and Nicole was playing attacker.

The Asteroids' coach put two substitutions on their front line. About two minutes into the second half, one of those new players streaked past Tess.

Faster, Tess told herself as she ran after her opponent. Her leg muscles cried out in protest. She tried her best to ignore the pain and catch up with the Asteroid. But the other player was fresher. She whipped past Tess and got off a solid pass to one of her teammates.

Seconds later, that teammate kicked a real zinger toward the Stars' goal—and scored.

"That's okay!" Tess called. "We're still ahead."

Tess felt how the effort of running without a break was draining the energy from her body. She knew her teammates must be feeling the same way. None of the girls were running as fast as they had been at the start of the game.

Toward the middle of the fourth quarter, Tess found herself battling an Asteroid for the ball. Tess turned around and dribbled the ball a few feet away from the Asteroid. Then she turned again and dribbled around her opponent.

"Smooth move," Tameka called out to Tess. "But watch out behind you."

Tess heard the sounds of another girl's footfalls

and her gasps for breath. She knew she had to pass, and she looked around. Out of the corner of her eye, she spotted Yasmine near the right-hand touchline. Open.

"Yaz!" Tess yelled as she got off a hard, fast pass. "Here's your chance."

Yasmine easily took control of the ball. She was in the perfect position to score and she knew it. Glancing quickly at the goal, Yasmine took aim and gave the ball a solid boot.

Tess immediately knew the ball was heading toward the goal at the wrong angle.

Yasmine saw it too. "No!" she cried as the goalkeeper moved into position to snatch the ball.

But then Jordan came sprinting forward. She kicked the ball as it bounced along the ground, giving it the extra force it needed to shoot powerfully into the back of the net. Goal!

Stars 3, Asteroids 1.

"Good one, Jordan!" Tess shouted.

"Yeah, that was really terrific. I don't know why I can't do that." Yasmine's voice was thick with frustration.

"Don't get bummed out," Jordan told Yasmine.

"You'll score soon. It's just that you're not used to playing the front line."

"Neither are you," Yasmine pointed out.

Jordan shrugged, looking almost apologetic for scoring.

"We've still got three minutes," Tess called forward to Yasmine as the girls lined up. "Try it again."

Tess saw Yasmine nod in agreement. But when the ref blew her whistle to signal the end of the game, Yasmine hadn't had another shot at goal. Still, Tess was glad the game was over. She was exhausted.

With the rest of the team, Tess stepped forward to shake hands with the girls on the other team. "Good game, good game," she murmured as she moved down the line of Asteroids.

Tess waited for Tameka to make her way through the line too. Then she threw one arm around her best friend's shoulders. "We won!" Tess said happily.

"I know!" Tameka said.

"Aren't you happy?" Tess asked.

Tameka nodded. "I scored two goals. That felt pretty good."

Tess drew away and gave her friend a playful punch in the arm. "I bet it did! But don't get too full of yourself. I'm going to score *at least* two goals in the next game."

"You're dreaming!" Tameka said.

Tess laughed. She didn't feel tired anymore. She felt terrific.

But a second later, Tess noticed Geena. She was sitting alone on the sidelines, watching her teammates celebrate. *Don't feel guilty,* Tess ordered herself, quickly looking away.

A few little lies were no big deal. Especially not if they helped the Stars win.

GEENA STOOD UP WITH A SIGH. THE game was over, and nobody had asked her to model for *Fourteen*. Actually, as far as she could tell, Tess's aunt had never even showed up. All the adults at the game looked familiar—and not nearly glamorous enough to work at *Fourteen*.

I wonder what happened to her? Geena thought glumly. She was beginning to feel stupid wearing her soccer uniform with makeup and hair spray. And she felt as if she'd let down the team by not playing.

Tameka dragged herself away from the water cooler and plopped down next to Geena. She began unlacing her cleats. The rest of the team was scattered around the field, getting ready to head out to the ice cream parlor.

"Good game, Tameka," Geena said dully. "You made three goals, right?"

"Nope—just two." Tameka cast a sideways looked at Geena. "Are you okay? You seem bummed out."

"I was just hoping that Tess's aunt . . . ," Geena started. She let her voice trail off when Rose stomped up to them with a furious look on her face.

"Is it true?" Rose demanded. "Is the game really over?"

Tameka and Geena looked at each other.

"It's true," Geena said. "We started at one. Did you forget?"

"No, I . . ." Rose narrowed her eyes at Geena. "You don't look like *you've* been playing."

"Well, I sat out," Geena said, feeling foolish all over again. "But the game is really over. Look at Tameka."

Rose took in Tameka's uniform, which was soggy with sweat, and her legs, which were smeared with mud. Then she let out a huge sigh. "I can't believe I missed the game," Rose said. "I thought I was going to be early."

"Early?" Tameka said as she strapped on her sandals. "Didn't anybody call you about the time change?"

"Yes," Rose said. "But I must have written down the wrong time. I could have sworn Tess said three o'clock."

"Tess?" Geena said, surprised. *Tess talked me out of playing this game, too.*

Tameka stood up, brushed off her legs, and picked up her cleats. "You guys are coming to Tosca's, right?" she asked.

Geena shrugged. "I guess."

"Sure," Rose said. "But I feel funny celebrating a game I didn't even *see*."

"Don't be too disappointed," Tameka said. "There's always next week. See you in a few minutes!"

Rose and Geena watched as Tameka headed across the field toward her parents.

"I can't believe I missed the game," Rose said sadly. "I'm so clueless sometimes. Oh well. Want to go see if we can grab a ride with Sarah?"

"Sarah isn't here," Geena said.

"Really?" Rose looked surprised.

"Really," Geena said, suddenly realizing that all

three of the beginners on the Stars' team had missed the same game. That seemed too convenient to be a coincidence.

"Wanna see if Tameka's parents can give us a ride?" Rose asked.

Geena shook her head. "No, let's walk. I think we've got something important to discuss. And we'd better do it in private."

★

"Hey, Sarah. It's me, Geena."

Geena had never spoken to any of her teammates on the phone before, and she felt kind of shy. "Rose is here too," she added, smiling at the redhead, who was sitting across from her at the Di Gregorios' cluttered kitchen table.

"I'm so glad you guys called!" Sarah's friendly tone immediately relaxed Geena. "How was the game this afternoon?"

"Well, we won."

"Great! Did you guys make any decent plays?"

"No. . . . Actually, neither of us played." Geena felt her face heat up. In the few hours since the game had ended, she'd become convinced that Tess's story about *Fourteen* was completely made up. Geena felt ashamed—and angry—that she'd allowed herself to be tricked.

"Why didn't you play?" Sarah sounded surprised.

"That's why we were calling you," Geena said. "Um, Rose and I were wondering—what happened to you today? Marina said you had some sort of appointment."

"I went to a play with my friend Jeff," Sarah said.

Geena's eyebrows shot up. "A date?"

Rose immediately looked more alert. "Who went on a date?" she asked.

Geena held up a finger. *Wait,* she mouthed.

"Not exactly," Sarah was saying. "I mean, Jeff's mom and dad were there. We went to see his sister in a play. It was kind of like a family outing."

"Still . . . ," Geena said.

"Trust me, it was no big deal," Sarah insisted. "I mean, I don't even *like* Jeff that much. I'm sure I would have had more fun at the game."

"So why didn't you come?" Geena asked.

Sarah sighed. "I'm not sure. Well, I guess it was because Lacey and Tess convinced me that going to the play might change my life. But I—"

"Tess!" Geena practically shouted.

"Um, yeah. So?" Now Sarah sounded really confused.

"Well, that's why I'm calling." Geena paused long enough to take a deep breath. "One of our teammates is up to no good. And we've got to stop her!"

★

"I'm absolutely positive I'm going to score a goal in this game," Yasmine told her mother the following Saturday afternoon. "So please, please, please watch me."

"Yeah," Yago chimed in from the backseat. "You wouldn't want to miss a miracle."

Yasmine gritted her teeth.

"I'll do my best, Yasmine," Mrs. Madrigal promised as she turned her sedan into the parking lot at the Beachside playing fields. "But remember, I've got to watch two games at the same time. Don't be too disappointed if I miss a play or two."

Yasmine climbed out of the car. "I don't mind if you miss a play or two," she said. "Just don't miss any *goals*."

"Don't miss any of mine, either!" Yago said.

Mrs. Madrigal popped opened the trunk.

Mr. Madrigal walked around to the back of the

96

car and pulled out a small cooler and the video camera.

"Ready," he said.

"Ready," Mrs. Madrigal echoed.

Good, Yasmine thought. She was ready too. Ready to score.

"This is more like it!" Marina said just before the game started. "I'm glad all the Stars are here today."

The Stars were playing the Galaxy that afternoon—the same team that had beaten them in their first game. Tess knew the Galaxy had a lot of strong players. *We'd have a better chance of beating them if Sarah, Rose, and Geena weren't playing,* Tess told herself. But Tess hadn't dared try to fool her teammates again. Partly because she'd felt too mean. But mostly because of Geena.

Geena hadn't said anything specific that worried Tess. In fact, on Tuesday at practice, she'd just nodded when Tess told her that her aunt had gotten lost on the way to Beachside. But still . . . something about the way Geena looked at her made Tess uncomfortable.

Marina tossed Jordan the multicolored goalkeeper's jersey. "Can you handle it?" she asked.

Jordan nodded in her quiet, confident way.

"Great," Marina said. "Nicole, left defender. Tameka, right defender."

Tameka made a face at Tess.

Tess knew her best friend didn't like playing defensive positions any more than she did. But she had to admit that Tameka had already spent her fair share of time in the front line.

"Geena, left midfielder," Marina went on. "Fiona, play in the center midfield. And Sarah, right midfielder."

Tess knew that Marina always had the front center be captain for the day. Since Tess had already had her turn as captain, it was unlikely that Marina would give her that position again. *So I'll play left or right attacker,* Tess thought.

"Rose, left attacker," Marina said. "Amber, right attacker. And, Yasmine, you're our center attacker and captain for the day."

Tess's jaw dropped. *What about me?* she thought. How could Marina not start her when she was one of the best girls on the team? The thought of starting the game sitting on the sidelines was depressing.

"All right!" Yasmine exclaimed. "Thanks for giving me another chance on the front line, Marina. I know I'm going to score today."

"You don't have to thank me," Marina said. "Everyone is going to get an equal chance to play each position. But good luck in scoring today."

"Cheer for us," Tameka said as she headed out to the field.

"I will." Tess forced a smile to hide her disappointment.

★

About two minutes into the first half, Fiona booted the ball toward the front line. The ball arced through the air, high above the players' heads.

Even when Fiona is playing midfield, she has a defender's kick, Yasmine thought with amusement. She knew from personal experience how hard it was to learn a new position. Like Fiona, Yasmine seemed to lack the careful aim that was so important to scoring goals.

"It's mine. Mine!" Yasmine judged where the ball would come down and then dashed forward. She kept her eye on the ball as it fell, fell, fell.

Yasmine dared a quick look toward the sidelines.

She wanted to make sure her parents were watching this play. Yasmine didn't see her father, but she spotted her mother easily. Mrs. Madrigal was standing near the Galaxy goal, the video camera pressed to her eye. The only problem was that she was taping Yago's game!

"Mom!" Yasmine called. "Mom, over here."

Yasmine was gratified when she saw her mother snap toward her. Without removing the camera from her eye, Mrs. Madrigal stalked a few feet closer to *her* touchline.

Good, Yasmine thought. *Now my first goal of the season will be on tape. I'll be able to show it to my grandchildren—and prove to Yago that I made it.*

Yasmine looked back up in the air, ready now to stop the ball. But the ball was gone! In fact, the only players in Galaxy territory were that team's goalkeeper and two defenders. Confused, Yasmine spun around. She saw one of the Galaxy midfielders driving the ball up the center of the field.

I missed the entire play, Yasmine thought with disgust. *How could I be so dumb?* But then she felt her temper flare. *This is all Yago's fault,* she told herself.

chapter 11

AT HALFTIME, THE SCORE WAS 2 TO 1. Galaxy was winning.

"I'd like you to go in as center midfielder," Marina told Tess. The coach also put Lacey in as right defender and had Nicole and Amber switch positions.

"All right, you guys, let's do it," Tess cheered. She had spent the entire first half evaluating what the Stars were doing wrong. It wasn't hard to see that some of her teammates weren't concentrating on the game. Rose, who was playing left attacker, kept spacing out. And Yasmine, usually a strong player, wasn't much more alert that afternoon.

The midfield wasn't that terrific, either. Sarah

and Geena had allowed several passes to get by them during the first half.

Well, some changes are about to be made, Tess thought. As the Stars took the field, Tess motioned for Rose, Yasmine, and Nicole to gather round.

"We're a goal behind," Tess reminded the others. "If we want to win this game, we've got to turn things around now."

"We're doing our best," Nicole told Tess.

"Well, our best isn't good enough," Tess said. "We've got to do even better."

Rose put her hands on her hips. "Are you saying we're not good enough to be on the team?"

Tess blinked in surprise. Rose was usually so meek.

"That's not what I meant," Tess said quickly. "I'm just saying that some of us play better than others—"

"Of course you're better than I am," Rose snapped. "You've been playing since you were in diapers. *I'm* just learning."

"That's my point," Tess said, forcing herself to be patient. "So if it gets tricky during this half, just get out of my way. I'll take care of things."

"Girls, cut the chatter!" Marina called from the sidelines. "Let's get into position!"

Tess shook her head as she lined up. She didn't understand why Rose and Nicole were giving her such a hard time when all she was trying to do was make sure that the Stars won.

Galaxy had the kickoff. Their center passed the ball to their left attacker, who started to dribble it into Star territory. Rose tried to cover the Galaxy attacker—but the attacker easily faked her out and continued down the field.

"I'm on her!" Geena called.

She must be terrified, Tess thought. "Come on, Geena. Get the ball. Use your feet," she reminded her.

Geena placed herself in front of the attacker. The second she got her foot on the ball, she kicked it over the touchline.

"Yay, Geena!" peeped a tiny voice from the sidelines.

Tess glanced over and saw one of Geena's little brothers watching them and clapping. She wished she could tell the peanut that kicking the ball out of bounds wasn't exactly something to be proud of—but he probably wouldn't care. Geena's little brothers and sisters seemed to think she was great no matter how badly she played.

"Throw-in—Galaxy!" the ref called, motioning toward the Stars' goal.

The Galaxy wing stepped over the touchline and picked up the ball. She pulled the ball behind her head and quickly threw to one of her teammates in the middle of the field.

Tess put on a burst of speed and got to the ball a moment after the Galaxy player did.

The girls battled for control.

"I'm open on your right!" Nicole hollered.

But Tess couldn't see Nicole. The Galaxy player was doing her best to block Tess's view of the field.

Finally Tess managed to draw the ball away from the Galaxy player with her right foot. Then she booted it toward Nicole with her left.

The Galaxy player immediately backed off, and Tess saw that her pass had been bad. The ball was bouncing across the field toward the touchline, several feet from where Nicole was waiting.

Nicole dashed after the ball. But she couldn't get to it before it rolled out of bounds.

"I was open!" Nicole yelled at Tess.

"I was aiming for you!" Tess shouted back.

"Could have fooled me," Nicole called.

Tess shook her head. *You'd think* she *never made a bad pass,* she thought.

"Throw-in—Galaxy!" the ref announced.

The Galaxy player who took the throw-in slipped at the last moment, and the ball plopped onto the grass just inside the touchline. Players from both teams ran to fight for the ball. To Tess's surprise, Sarah got control and awkwardly started to dribble the ball along the touchline.

"Go, Sarah!" Tess yelled encouragingly.

But then a Galaxy player challenged Sarah. She knocked the ball out of Sarah's control—and out of bounds. Sarah was nervous about making a mistake, so Tess took the throw-in. She aimed for Yasmine, who was deep in Galaxy territory.

The throw was good. Yasmine drove the ball toward the Galaxy goal. The Galaxy goalkeeper held her arms out to the sides, ready for Yasmine's shot.

Off by a mile, Tess thought of Yasmine's attempt at the goal. But then she realized Yasmine wasn't shooting on the goal, she was *passing* to

Nicole. Nicole galloped forward and gently tapped the ball. The direction change was enough to throw off the goalkeeper, and the ball rolled into the net.

Goal! That brought the game to a tie.

Tess ran over to the other girls. "Great pass, Yaz. Way to go, Nicole!"

Nicole didn't return her smile. "Oh, so now I'm suddenly good enough to touch the ball?"

Tess felt her excitement vanish. She'd never said Nicole wasn't good enough to touch the ball. Why was Nicole always picking a fight with her?

★

The rest of the quarter was a blur for Geena. At one point the ball rolled directly to her and stopped. Geena immediately looked around for someone to pass to—but nobody seemed open. The Galaxy players were rushing toward her. *What do I do?* Geena thought in panic.

"Pass it here!" Tess hollered.

Geena quickly passed the ball to Tess. But she didn't kick it hard enough. Before Tess got control, a crowd of opponents swarmed around and fought for the ball. Geena saw Tess and one of the Galaxy girls fall down in a tangle. She watched helplessly as another Galaxy player drove the ball away from the huddle and into Star territory.

That was totally lame, Geena thought. But she felt better when her little brothers and sisters started cheering for her. Seven-year-old Naomi had elected herself head cheerleader.

"That's all right, that's okay—you'll do it right *someday!*" they chanted as loudly as they could.

Geena broke into a grin as she started to trot up field. *Oh well,* she told herself. *At least I'm playing in this game—instead of sitting on the sidelines looking like a cheerleader myself.*

During the substitution break, Marina caught Geena's eye over the heads of the other players. "I just asked Fiona to go in as left midfielder," the coach said. "You can relax for the rest of the game."

Geena felt a pang of disappointment. But she knew Marina's decision was fair. She'd already played more than half the game.

The rest of the Stars took their places on the field, and Geena found herself alone with Nicole on the sidelines.

Great, Geena thought. Nicole wasn't her favorite teammate. In fact, Geena had nicknamed her "the snob of the Stars." Not only did Nicole always wear expensive designer outfits to practices, she never spoke to any of the beginners. Geena thought Nicole wanted to be friends only with Yasmine, Tameka, and Tess—the best players on the team.

On the other hand, Geena had to admit she hadn't exactly tried to cultivate Nicole's friendship. *Maybe I'm not being fair,* Geena thought. *Maybe Nicole thinks* I'm *a snob.*

Geena cleared her throat. "Good game, huh?" she asked.

"It stinks!" Nicole's blue eyes were flashing. Her arms were crossed in front of her chest.

"Stinks?" Geena asked, startled. "Why?"

"I just spent the entire quarter running up and down the field," Nicole huffed. "And I only got the ball once! Of course you know what the problem is."

Geena didn't. She shook her head slightly.

"Tess!" Nicole bellowed. "She kicked the ball out of bounds instead of passing it to me. Did you see that?"

Geena thought back. She couldn't remember the play, but it didn't seem to matter. Nicole rushed on without waiting for her to answer.

"And later, when you had the ball," Nicole said. "She called for it even though Galaxy players were buzzing around her like flies! Meanwhile, guess who was wide open? Me!"

Geena thought that mistake sounded more like her own fault than Tess's. "Oops," Geena said. "Sorry."

"It's not *your* fault," Nicole insisted. "It's Tess's. She's the world's biggest ball hog."

Geena realized that she had been wrong about Nicole and Tess. They definitely *weren't* friends. Geena thought for a moment. Maybe Nicole could help her and Sarah and Rose.

"Ball hogging is not the worst of it," Geena told Nicole in a low voice. "I think Tess is trying to break up the team."

Nicole's eyebrows flew up. "Break up the team?"

Geena nodded solemnly. "Maybe you can help me think of a way to stop her."

"You bet I will!" Nicole said firmly.

★

Tess made her first goal of the day near the end of the second half with a scorching kick into the upper left-hand corner of the net. The Galaxy goalkeeper didn't even get close to it.

Stars 3, Galaxy 2.

Yasmine was glad the Stars had pulled into the lead. But she was more concerned with the clock. About three minutes were left in the game, she guessed. She didn't have much more time to score. Then she saw Rose dribbling the ball toward a wall of Galaxy players.

"I'm open," Yasmine yelled. "Pass it to your right, Rose."

Anxiously, Yasmine glanced toward the sidelines to make sure her parents were watching. But she saw the back of Mrs. Madrigal's ponytail. *She's taping Yago's game,* Yasmine thought with disgust. At the same moment Rose passed the ball in her direction with a good strong boot.

"Mom!" Yasmine shouted as loudly as she could.

She kept her eye on the ball until she had it firmly in control. Then she glanced at the sidelines. *Good,* she thought. *Mom is paying attention.*

Yasmine started to dribble toward the goal. The Galaxy defenders were still upfield. Yasmine was certain they wouldn't get to her in time to stop her from scoring. That meant that nothing stood between her and the goal except the Galaxy goalkeeper. This time Yasmine wouldn't be forced into kicking from a distance. She could take the ball right into the goal. *I can't miss,* she thought.

As Yasmine closed in on the goal she heard a familiar voice. It was Yago! And he was calling "Mom! Dad!"

No way, Yasmine thought. She peeked toward the sidelines. Sure enough, her mother and father were turning away—just as she was about to make her first goal of the season!

"Mom! Watch me!" Yasmine called frantically. She could hear the pounding of feet on the ground behind her. The defenders were coming.

Yasmine glanced toward the sidelines long enough to see her mother dash back toward the Stars' playing field. *Good,* she thought. Yasmine was about to turn her attention back to the goal when she noticed something that made her stop. The video camera was pressed firmly to her mother's eye as she ran—and she didn't seem aware that she was heading straight toward a Big Wheel that one of Geena's brothers or sisters had left near the touchline.

"Mom! Watch out!" Yasmine yelled.

But it was too late. Mrs. Madrigal ran into the

Big Wheel full tilt. Her body jerked forward and the video camera went flying through the air. She landed on her knees hard. Mr. Madrigal caught the camera just inches from the ground.

Abandoning the ball, Yasmine ran off the field. "Mom? Mom, are you okay?" she yelled as she dashed toward her mother, who was crumpled up on the grass.

The ref blew his whistle to signal stop of play. He ran over to the sidelines too. So did Marina, most of the Stars, and most of the Suns. The Galaxy players flopped down in the grass to rest.

Yago and Yasmine hovered over their mother.

"Mom, are you all right?" Yago asked.

"I—I think so," Mrs. Madrigal said. "But my ankle feels funny."

A man pushed through the crowd. Yasmine recognized Nicole's father. She knew he was a doctor. He knelt down to examine Mrs. Madrigal's ankle.

Please let her be okay, Yasmine thought.

"It's not broken," Nicole's father said. "It's not even sprained. Just bruised."

Whew! Yasmine thought.

"All right, let's finish up this game!" the ref said. "We'll start with a ball drop."

Yago fell into step with Yasmine as the players headed back to their fields. "I guess this means you haven't scored yet," he said.

Yasmine fought an urge to groan. For a moment, she'd forgotten. But her stupid twin brother was right. She had blown her chance to score. Again.

Nicole gave Sarah, Rose, and Geena a triumphant look. "Fiona is in," she announced, turning off her portable phone.

Geena looked down at the team list she was holding, and made a check mark next to Fiona's name. "That just leaves Yaz and Tameka," she said.

"You're really good at talking people into doing stuff, Nicole," Sarah told Nicole from her spot on the floor.

Nicole shrugged modestly. "Sneaky comes naturally to me."

Geena couldn't help nodding at that. Nicole was *outstanding* at sneaky. In just three days,

Nicole had formulated a plan for saving the team—and she was now putting the plan into action. Geena admired Nicole's cleverness, but it also frightened her. *I hope Nicole never gets mad at me,* Geena thought uneasily. But then she pushed that thought aside.

"Do you want Yaz's number next?" Geena asked.

"Um . . ." Nicole got up and padded across the thick white carpeting to a closet that ran along one side of her room. She took out a pink sweater and put it on. Nicole's parents kept the central air-conditioning in their house blasting, and it was freezing in Nicole's room. Geena's own arms were covered with goose bumps. She wished she had a sweater too.

"We're not going to call Yaz," Nicole said as she sat down next to the phone again.

Rose and Geena exchanged surprised looks.

"I thought the plan was to talk to the entire team," Geena said.

"That was the plan *yesterday,*" Nicole said. "But now I think telling Tameka and Yaz is too risky."

"Because they're Tess's friends?" Sarah asked.

"Exactly," Nicole said with a nod. "If they tell Tess about Operation Foul Play, everything will be ruined."

"What do you guys think?" Geena asked Rose and Sarah.

"Okay with me," Sarah said.

Rose shrugged. "It's Nicole's plan. I guess she knows best."

I hope you're right, Geena thought as she folded up the list of phone numbers. She kept wondering if it wouldn't be easier to just talk to Tess.

No, Geena told herself impatiently. *We've already discussed that a thousand times.* Nicole had finally convinced Geena and the others that talking was a waste of time. Tess wouldn't change just because they asked her to.

Operation Foul Play is the only way, Geena decided. *I just hope it works.*

Nicole smiled with satisfaction. "All we have to do now is wait until the game on Saturday," she said. "Then the moment Marina puts Tess into the game, we can put our plan into action."

★

"Great work," Marina said as the girls came off the field the following Saturday.

The Meteors had kept the Stars running during the first quarter. Now the girls eagerly crowded around the big cooler of water.

Tess thought the game was going well so far. Tameka had scored a goal early on. But then an oversized Meteor had tied up the game with a powerful boot into the Stars' goal. Tess could hardly wait to start playing. She'd been stuck on the sidelines since the game began. And so had Yasmine.

"You guys are really looking like a team out there," Marina continued. "I didn't see you bunch up once."

Nicole shot a look at Tess. "We're not *all* ball hogs," she said.

Tess frowned. "What's that supposed to mean?" she asked.

"Listen up for substitutions, everyone!" Marina called before Nicole could answer. "Tameka and Geena, you can cool your heels for a few minutes. Yaz, go in as center attacker. And Tess, take over as right attacker."

All right, Tess thought. *The front line.*

Nicole cleared her throat loudly. "Did you hear that, guys? *Tess is going in.*"

Tess and Tameka exchanged looks. Nicole was acting strange.

"Hey, Marina?" Fiona hung her head. "Would you mind taking me out? My allergies are bothering me."

Tess was surprised by Fiona's request. Fiona had looked really energetic playing left attacker during the first quarter. Tess hadn't seen her sneeze once.

"Sure," Marina said, looking concerned.

Tess thought she saw Nicole wink at Fiona. *What's going on?* she wondered with a frown.

The ref blew her whistle. "Let's go! Let's go!"

Marina pointed to Geena. "Okay, go in as left attacker."

But Geena suddenly bent over and grabbed her belly. "I can't," she said with a groan. "I have a stomachache."

"How much water did you drink?" Marina demanded.

"Four cups," Geena said.

Tess gave her teammate a surprised look. She had been standing right next to the cooler—and she knew Geena hadn't had more than two cups of water.

"Okay, have a seat," Marina told Geena. "And next time, take it easy with the water. That goes for all of you. Tameka, you're up! Take over as left attacker."

Tameka jumped to her feet.

"Marina?" Sarah said hesitantly. "I—um, I have to go to the bathroom."

"Now?" Marina raised her eyebrows. "Can't you hold it?"

Sarah made a face. "I can't. It's an emergency."

"Okay—go!" Marina told Sarah.

The tall girl trotted down the sidelines.

"Everybody else, hit the field," Marina said. "Jordan, you're going to have to play defender. Lacey and Amber, spread out in the midfield."

Mr. Thomas jogged over to the ref to tell her the Stars would be fielding only eight players.

Tameka quickly took her position at the left of the front line. "Are you ready to make your goal?" she asked Yasmine as the girls waited for the game to resume.

"You bet!" Yasmine replied.

"If we get the ball within shooting distance, I'll pass it to you," Tess said. "Just try to stay open."

Yasmine broke into a grin. "Deal!"

Seconds later the game got under way. Tess passed the ball left to Tameka. But a Meteor intercepted and kicked the ball out of bounds.

"Throw-in—Stars!"

Tameka quickly scooped up the ball and got ready to throw. She met Tess's eyes for a fraction of a second. *She's aiming it at me,* Tess thought. She bent her knees slightly and got ready to run.

"Hang on!" Marina called from the sidelines.

What now? Tess spun around to see what was holding up the game. Her impatience disappeared when she saw Nicole limping across Star territory toward Marina.

Nicole joined Geena and Fiona on the sidelines. Sarah still hadn't come back from the bathroom. As Marina and the ref started to confer, Tess wondered what was going on with her teammates. Had they been struck by some mysterious illness?

Yasmine walked over to Tess and sat down right in the middle of the field. Tess plopped down next to her. Tameka came over too.

Lacey headed toward the sidelines.

"Are you going to find out what's going on?" Yasmine called to her.

Lacey shook her head. "I feel like I'm going to throw up," she said.

Tess, Yasmine, and Tameka looked at each other.

"What's wrong with everybody?" Yasmine asked.

Tameka shrugged. "I don't know, but there's only six of us left," she said. "Do you think the ref will let the game go on? It wouldn't exactly be fair."

"We could still win," Tess said.

The ref trotted back across the field.

"Tameka!" Marina said. "Play defender."

Tess smiled. "It looks like we get to play," she said happily.

Tameka jumped up and ran back toward the goal.

Yasmine got to her feet slowly. "I guess I'm not going to get a goal now," she said.

"Why not?" Tess asked.

"Because there are three more Meteors than Stars on the field!" Yasmine exclaimed. "We're probably not even going to get *close* to their goal."

"Sure we are," Tess said. "We'll just have to play harder."

It wasn't that simple.

The Meteors were everywhere. Anytime one of the Stars got the ball, a Meteor—or two—appeared out of nowhere to cover her. And dribbling against two opponents was practically impossible.

"Finally!" Yasmine exclaimed when the ref signaled the end of the half. "I hope we get some help now."

★

"Sarah, I want you to go in as right defender . . ." Marina let her voice trail off as her eyes skipped from face to face. "Where *is* Sarah? Didn't she come back from the bathroom?"

"I don't think so," Nicole said.

Marina frowned. "That's strange. Nicole, would you please go look for her?"

"Sure," Nicole said. She got up, and skipped off toward the bathrooms.

Her leg looks fine now, Tess thought with a frown. She couldn't shake the feeling that something strange was going on with her teammates. But what?

"Let's see . . ." Marina made some changes to her team lineup, which she had sketched out on a piece of yellow paper. "Fiona, why don't you go in as defender?"

"Um—I'd better not," Fiona said. "My breathing isn't that good."

Marina looked up from her list. "Lacey?"

"My stomach still hurts."

"Mine hurts too. I don't think I can go back in," Amber said.

Marina folded up her lineup and put it back in her pocket. She chewed on her lip—and seemed about to say something. But then she sighed.

"Okay," the coach said. "I can't make you play if you don't want to. How about if you each take the same position you had?" Marina made it sound more like a question than an order.

"But there's only five of us," Yasmine protested.

"I know," Marina said. "Rose, why don't you come out of the goal? You and Jordan can cover the backfield. Tameka, Yaz, and Tess, play forward."

Marina and Mr. Thomas headed over to the ref, who was standing with the Meteors' coach. The four of them began a hurried, whispered conversation.

Tess got to her feet with a feeling of unreality.

Six of her teammates couldn't *all* be hurt or sick. But why on earth would they drop out of the game on purpose?

As the others trooped onto the field, Tess paused in front of Amber, who was perched on a root of the oak tree. "Are you *sure* you have a stomachache?" Tess asked. "Because we could really use you on the field."

Amber's gaze darted toward Geena, who was sitting nearby.

Geena shook her head slightly, and Amber dropped her eyes to the ground. "I'm sure," she whispered.

"Fine!" Tess turned and stomped onto the field. She didn't like mysteries, and her teammates seemed to be involved in one.

YASMINE AND TAMEKA LOOKED JUST AS baffled as Tess felt.

"Any idea what we do now?" Yasmine asked as Tess joined them on the front line.

"Run as fast as you can," Tameka said with a sour laugh.

Tess saw the Meteors exchanging looks. Clearly, they were surprised that the Stars were fielding only five players. *Maybe they'll get too relaxed*, Tess thought without hope.

"The Stars are—um, unable to field the minimum of seven players required for a game," the confused-looking ref announced. "But your coaches want you to continue playing. If any of you Stars get too tired to go on, let me know."

The Stars nodded, and the ref signaled the beginning of the second half. Tess tried to shake off her frustration and focus on the game.

The Meteor center passed to her left attacker. Tess immediately started trying to steal the ball from her.

Tameka covered the Meteors' center attacker. Yasmine was sticking close to the right attacker. But there were too many Meteors for a real defense.

The Meteors quickly drove into Star territory and got dangerously close to scoring. But Jordan shut them down by lofting the ball out of bounds.

"Throw-in—Meteors!"

A Meteor midfielder grabbed the ball and positioned herself on the touchline. Tameka and Yasmine ran over to cover the throw.

"This couldn't get worse," Yasmine groused.

The ref held up a hand. "Hang on," she told the Meteor midfielder. "I think we have a substitution."

"Yippee!" Tess said. "Maybe we're getting some reinforcements."

Tess couldn't believe her eyes when exactly the

opposite turned out to be true. Jordan and Rose were *both* heading for the sidelines.

"What is going on?" Tess yelled.

"Your team is deserting you," the Meteor midfielder told her with a grin. "And we're going to beat the pants off you."

Tess felt her competitive juices start to flow faster. "Oh yeah? Let's see you!"

Tess, Yasmine, and Tameka did their best to handle the entire field. But three players didn't have a hope against nine.

By the time the quarter ended, Tess's jersey was soaked through with sweat. Blood was pumping through her veins so hard that her skin had turned beet red. She considered it a victory that she, Yasmine, and Tameka had allowed the Meteors to score only one goal during the quarter.

"You okay?" Tameka asked as they walked off the field.

Tess just nodded. Her throat was sore from panting hard.

Yasmine trudged along silently next to the others.

Tess wasn't looking forward to getting to the sidelines and facing the rest of the Stars. Those girls were just sitting there and watching while their teammates practically killed themselves on the field.

"How could they desert us like this?" Tess asked Yasmine and Tameka. "We're supposed to be a team! Nobody can convince me they're all really sick."

Marina was waiting for the girls by the touch-line. She put a hand on Tess's shoulder.

"It's over," the coach said to the three players, but loud enough for the entire team to hear. "You're pushing yourselves too hard out there, and I can't let it continue."

Tess shook off Marina's hand. "This stinks!" she shouted. "I don't understand why we have to quit when we have eight perfectly healthy players just sitting around."

Tess faced her teammates, who were spread out over the grassy sidelines. "Come on, you guys," she pleaded. "We need you out there. I can't win this game all by myself, you know!"

Nicole stood up and met Tess's gaze evenly. "*We* know that, but do you?"

"I thought you liked to play alone," Sarah said in a quiet voice.

"No!" Tess insisted. "Soccer is a team sport. I need help!"

"If you want help, then you're going to have to accept it from *all* of us," Geena said. "You can't pick and choose the teammates you think are good enough."

"What are you talking about?" Tess demanded. Her heart was still beating hard—only now it was from fear, not exertion.

"Tess, we know you lied to us," Rose said, not raising her voice. "We know you told me the wrong game time on purpose."

"And made up that dumb story about *Fourteen*," Geena put in.

"I—I was just trying to help us win!" Tess shot back. "That's what we all want. Right, Yasmine?"

Yasmine briefly met Tess's gaze.

Come on, Tess urged her silently. *Be honest. Tell them you agree with me.* Tess's heart sank when Yasmine began to shake her head slowly.

"Winning really isn't that important to me," Yasmine said. "All I want to do is learn how to be a good attacker. And that's easier to do when everybody is working together—not when one player is trying to be a star."

Tess felt almost dizzy. She was surprised that her teammates were making her seem so *evil*.

She shot a quick glance at Marina. The coach was standing with her arms crossed, carefully listening to what the girls were saying but not interfering—yet.

Tess spun around to face the one person she knew would stand by her. "Tameka," she pleaded. "Tell them I just did it for the team's sake."

Tameka took a deep breath. "I can't," she whispered.

The blood was roaring in Tess's ears. She couldn't believe that the entire team had turned on her. Even her best friend. Tess felt numb.

"Are you guys still interested in playing?" the ref called.

Marina gave the girls a questioning look. "How about it? Are you guys a team—or not?"

"Yes!" Geena said firmly.

"I think at least *ten* of us are," Nicole said, shooting a poisonous look at Tess.

"Do you want to play?" Marina asked.

"Yes," the girls said, all at once. Tess was the only one who didn't answer.

"We're playing!" Marina shouted to the ref.

"I'll give you thirty seconds," the ref called back.

"Tess, I want to talk to you," Marina said crisply. "Yasmine and Tameka, I think you've seen enough action for one game. Everyone else, get ready to hit the field." As the coach quickly ran through the lineup, Tess sat down on the aluminum bench. Her chest felt hollow, and each beat of her heart was painful.

Tameka crouched down in front of the bench. "Tess—you okay?"

"Sure." Sudden tears rushed to Tess's eyes. She knew if she tried to say anything more, the tears would flood out. *I am not going to cry,* Tess told herself fiercely. She didn't want her teammates to know how badly they'd hurt her.

As soon as the game got under way, Marina came over. "Tameka," she said. "If you don't mind, I'd like to talk to Tess privately for a few minutes."

"Oh, no problem." Tameka hurriedly stood up and went to sit with Yasmine several yards away.

I guess we're not friends anymore, Tess thought miserably. *Tameka would never want to be friends with a liar.*

"Why don't you tell me what happened?" Marina said gently.

"I did just what they said," Tess said dully. "I tried to keep Sarah, Geena, and Rose out of our second game, the one against the Asteroids."

"Why?" Marina asked.

"I wanted to win."

"What about last week's game and this one?" Marina asked.

"What about them?" Tess didn't understand what Marina wanted to know.

"Did you try to keep Sarah, Geena, and Rose from playing in them?" Marina said.

"No."

"Why not?"

"I don't know," Tess said with a shrug. "I thought they would figure out what I was doing. And . . . well, I just didn't feel like lying to them again."

Tess pressed her hands together. She didn't expect the coach to understand what she had done—or have any sympathy for her. After all, Marina didn't care about winning.

An eternity seemed to pass before Marina spoke. "You know, Tess, what you did—discouraging the worst players, making sure the Stars had the best possible chance to win—that's exactly how some people would define good coaching."

"Not you," Tess said.

Marina smiled slightly. "No, not me."

"But why not?" Tess wailed. "What's so bad about winning?"

"There's nothing *bad* about winning," Marina said slowly. "It's just that winning isn't as important as lots of other things. Like making friends, learning new skills, exercising, and mastering good sportsmanship. I think most of your teammates would agree with what Yasmine said earlier. They just don't care about winning."

This didn't make sense to Tess. "If you don't want to win, what's the point?" she asked.

"The point is to *participate*," Marina said. "Listen, your teammates may not play soccer as well as you do, but they're not stupid. They know that if the Stars made it a priority to win every game, some of them would never get to play. Try, just for a second, to put yourself in their position. How do you feel when you're on the sidelines?"

"Bored."

"Geena and Sarah and Rose feel the same way."

"I guess," Tess said slowly. She was waiting for Marina to tell her she was off the team.

A roar of approval erupted from the crowd of fans.

"What happened?" Marina called to Tameka and Yasmine.

"Geena just scored," Tameka answered.

"Her family is going nuts," Yasmine added.

Marina leaped to her feet and started to applaud. "Way to go, Geena!" she whooped. Marina turned back to Tess. "That was Geena's first goal of the season! She's really learned a lot in a few weeks."

"Yeah—it's great," Tess said. "But, Marina, what about me and, um—my punishment?"

"Oh." Marina's face grew serious. "Sit out the rest of the game and think about what you did."

Tess spent the rest of the game alone on the bench. Lacey scored just before the end of the quarter. The Stars ended up winning 3 to 2. But Tess knew she wouldn't be welcome at the celebration after the game. By the time the team came off the field, she was already gone.

chapter 14

WHEN TESS GOT HOME, HER HOUSE WAS empty. She wasn't surprised. Saturday was a big day for real estate. Her mother usually had at least one open house.

Tess dragged herself upstairs to her room. She plopped down on the bed and relived the scene at the soccer field in her mind. This time, when her eyes filled up with tears, she let them fall.

What hurt most was that Tameka and Yasmine hadn't stood by her. *I wish I had never come up with that plan,* Tess thought. *Winning one stupid game wasn't worth losing all my friends.*

A knock on her door startled her. She quickly

sat up and batted at her tears. "Mom—is that you?"

The door opened a crack. "No, it's me. Tameka."

"What are you doing here?" Tess demanded.

"I came to see if you were all right." Tameka stepped into the room. She had changed out of her sweaty uniform and let her braids down from their ponytail.

"Why?" Tess asked. "I thought you hated me."

Tameka made a get-real face. "No way—you're my best friend."

Tess felt an enormous surge of relief. But then she thought of Yasmine—and all the other Stars. "Well, everyone else hates me," she said.

Tameka sat down on the edge of the bed. "I don't think they *hate* you. They're just a little angry. But if you apologized, I'm sure—"

"I can't!" Tess interrupted. "I can't go to practice and face the team—*and* Marina. No way."

"Well, then what are you going to do?" Tameka asked.

Tess considered for a moment. "I guess—I guess I'm going to quit."

"You *can't*," Tameka said forcefully.

"Why not? Nobody wants me around."

"Because you *love* soccer," Tameka said. "If you stopped playing, you'd probably shrivel up and die."

Tess cracked a smile, but Tameka's expression was serious.

"Besides," Tameka went on, "I'd miss you. The whole team would miss you."

"I seriously doubt that!"

"It's true," Tameka said. "Sometimes you're a pain in the neck. And sometimes you go too far. But we need you. You're our leader, and leaders don't quit."

Tess felt her throat tighten up. A leader—she hadn't thought about it that way before. But she had helped Sarah learn to dribble and helped Rose learn not to duck when the ball headed her way. Somewhere along the line, though, she had decided *winning* was more important than *leading*.

But was it really? Tameka didn't think so. And neither did Marina. But Tess wasn't so sure she agreed with them.

Tess studied Tameka's face for a moment longer. "I'll think about it," she promised.

★

"Meeki?" Tess said into the phone on Thursday afternoon. "It's me. Tess."

"No duh!" Tameka was laughing. "You're the only person in the world who calls me Meeki!"

Tess was too keyed up to joke around. "What are you doing?"

"Getting ready for practice."

Tess took a deep breath. "Can your dad give me a ride."

"Sure!"

"Don't ask him if you think being seen with me will make the other girls hate you," Tess added in a rush.

Tameka sighed. "Don't be stupid. We'll pick you up in ten minutes."

Tess went outside. She sat down on her front steps to wait for Tameka and Mr. Thomas. But a second later she jumped up again, too nervous to sit still. Her teammates had sent her a message on Saturday: Get lost! The Stars had made it crystal clear that they didn't want to play with her anymore. But missing practice on Tuesday had made Tess super-miserable. So she had screwed up her courage and decided to see what happened if she showed up at the field. *Don't wimp out now,* Tess ordered herself.

A few minutes later, Tess relaxed slightly when

she saw Mr. Thomas's car pull up in front of her house. Facing the team would be much easier with her best friend's support.

Marina was standing on the sidelines when Mr. Thomas, Tess, and Tameka arrived at the field. "Hi, guys," she greeted the girls. "Why don't you each grab a ball? Warm up by trying to dribble it on your thighs."

At least Marina doesn't seem surprised to see me, Tess told herself. She got a ball and followed Tameka onto the field, where the rest of the team had already gathered.

"Hi!" Tameka called out.

"Hi," Tess mumbled.

The other girls returned their greetings. Some looked friendlier than others. Geena made a point of giving Tess a big smile. But Yasmine seemed embarrassed. And Nicole was scowling.

Tess smiled back at Geena. Then she turned away from the other girls and tried to concentrate on warming up. *I can't force them to be nice to me,* Tess told herself.

After everyone's muscles were good and warm, Marina showed the girls the drill she wanted them to do that day. Tameka and Tess were partners as usual. And although the friends chatted between themselves, the other girls kept their distance.

Tess noticed that Sarah was starting to dribble with the outside of her foot. She began to praise her teammate, but then bit her tongue. *Sarah will just think I'm trying to suck up,* Tess thought.

"Let's scrimmage!" Marina called out about twenty minutes before practice ended. She quickly assigned sides. Tess ended up on a team with Nicole, Amber, Sarah, and Rose.

"Okay, get together with your team and decide who's going to play what," Marina said.

Scrimmaging was Tess's favorite part of practice. Usually she couldn't wait for the mini-game to begin. She liked to take control of her team and get them organized quickly, so there wasn't any delay.

But now Tess slowly dragged herself over to where her team had gathered. *Why couldn't I be on the same team as Tameka?* she wondered.

"Everyone tell me what they want to play," Nicole said briskly as Tess joined the other girls.

"Attacker," Amber said.

"Attacker," Sarah said.

"Defender," Rose said.

Nicole didn't wait for Tess's response. "I want to be an attacker," she announced. "So let's do this. Amber can play midfield. Sarah and I will play forward. Rose, you play defender. And Tess, goalkeeper."

Amber, Rose, and Sarah glanced at Tess. Tess knew they were interested in how she was going to react to Nicole's bossy behavior—and the fact that Nicole wanted her to play goalkeeper, a position she hated.

Tess just turned and headed toward the goal.

She told Tameka about what Nicole had done in the car on the way home. "I can't believe she made me play goalkeeper. She might as well have said go away!" Tess sighed heavily. "I feel like everyone on the team wants me to disappear."

"I bet Rose felt the same way when you told her the wrong game time," Tameka said.

Tess blinked with surprise. But then she nodded. *Poor Rose,* she thought.

"Today is the day," Yasmine told Tameka at the Stars' game on Saturday. "I'm going to score. I can feel it."

"You're definitely ready," Tameka agreed with a smile.

"Absolutely," Tess put in.

"I hope you're right," Yasmine said.

Showing up for the game that afternoon had been difficult for Tess. Especially after most of her teammates had given her the cold shoulder at practice. Tess was worried that nobody would pass her the ball during the game. *If that happens, I'll have to quit,* Tess thought. But she hoped that wouldn't be necessary.

Tess was just grateful that Yasmine was talking to her again. *Two down, eight to go,* she told herself with a wry smile.

About five minutes before game time, Marina called the girls together to hear the day's lineup. "Sarah, I'd like you to play goalkeeper today," the coach said. "You've made some great saves in practice, so I'm sure you'll do a good job."

Sarah nodded.

"Lacey, left defender," Marina continued to read from her list. "Nicole, center defender. Yasmine, right defender."

Tess saw Yasmine's shoulders slump. *That's a tough break,* she thought. *Yasmine was all fired up to score. And she's not going to be able to do that playing defense.*

Marina told Tameka to play center attacker. She would also be captain for the day. "And Tess, you'll start as right attacker," Marina finished up.

Tess knew that she and Tameka played well together. With the two of them on the front line, the Stars had a good chance of winning.

"Marina?" Tess said half a heartbeat later.

"Yes?"

"Why don't you let Yasmine play right attacker?" Tess suggested. "Because, um, she has a lucky feeling that today's going to be the day she scores. And, well, I'm really in the mood to play defense."

Marina winked at Tess. "Sounds reasonable to me."

Yasmine held out a hand, and Tess gave her a high five. "Thanks," Yasmine said simply. Then she trotted off to take her position.

Tameka gave Tess a funny look. "Since when do you get in the mood to play *defense*? You hate defense."

"Not today!"

chapter 15

RELAX, RELAX, RELAX, YASMINE TOLD herself as she walked toward her position on the front line. She knew if she wanted to score, she had to stay calm.

Tameka and the Asteroids' center stepped forward for the coin toss.

Yasmine glanced toward the sidelines. She immediately spotted her parents. Yasmine gave her mom and dad a thumbs-up and tried to think confident thoughts.

About twenty minutes into the half, Fiona was putting the pressure on the Asteroids' right defender. The Asteroid panicked and dumped the ball into an open space in the center of the field.

"Mine!" Tess hollered. She jumped up and stopped the ball with her inner thigh. Quickly getting the ball under control, Tess dribbled toward the halfway line. She gained several yards before an Asteroid started to close in.

Waiting until the last safe second, Tess booted a scorching pass to Geena, who was wide open.

Beautiful, Yasmine thought as she ran up the touchline.

Geena let the ball bounce in front of her. She chased it into Asteroid territory, controlling the ball as best she could. She was only a few yards from the goal when two Asteroid defenders started to put the pressure on. Geena needed to pass.

Yasmine was in position.

Geena booted an angled pass her way.

Yasmine ran forward. She carefully timed her approach so that she would connect with the ball just in front of the goal.

The goalkeeper started to step toward the left side of her goal area. Yasmine saw her. So she kicked the ball with the top of her foot—firing it like a cannonball directly into the net.

The goalkeeper went for it. But she was too late.

"Goal—Stars!"

Yasmine had never heard sweeter words.

She couldn't wait to tell Yago about her goal. Over and over again. In detail. Until he felt as if he wanted to scream. She'd make him wish he'd never bet she couldn't make a goal.

★

"Beautiful goal!" Marina said to Yasmine as the Stars came off the field at halftime.

"Flawless," Tess put in.

Amber started to fill up cups of water. "Pass these around," she said.

"I'm so happy you finally got your goal," Sarah told Yasmine.

Yasmine smiled self-consciously. "Well, Geena helped. She got the ball into Asteroid territory and then passed it right to me."

Nicole handed a cup of water to Tess.

"Thanks," Tess said, surprised by the friendly gesture.

Nicole shrugged. "No big deal."

"I couldn't have gotten the ball in front of the goal alone," Geena said. "I mean, I was mostly just chasing after that blistering pass from Tess."

Sarah rolled her eyes. "Nobody wants to take

credit! Who are *you* going to thank, Tess? The Asteroid who missed her pass?"

"No," Tess said with a laugh. "Instead I'm going to propose a toast." She raised her cup of water and waited until the rest of the Stars did the same. "To teamwork!" Tess said.

"Teamwork," Marina, Mr. Thomas and the Stars echoed.

Tess smiled. She was beginning to realize just what that word meant.

Soccer Tips from

DRIBBLING

Dribbling is one of the most important parts of soccer. It allows you to slow down play while your teammates maneuver into good positions. Dribbling is also used when you have an open field and want to move the ball closer to the goal to get into scoring position. Tactical use of dribbling can mean the difference between a good game and a great game.

Dribbling requires constant awareness of the field and attention to the ball. To split your focus between the ball at your feet and the rest of the players, you need to concentrate. Once you learn the basic technique, you'll have the freedom to scan the field because you'll know exactly where the ball is without looking.

The most important thing to remember about dribbling is to keep the ball close enough to you so that an opposing player can't take it away. But you still want to keep the ball moving forward and run with it. Here's what you do:

- Keep your body bent slightly forward, turning one shoulder toward the defender's chest to shield the ball.
- To move the ball, use the top, bottom, inside, and outside of the foot farther from your opponent. If

there's no pressure from an oncoming opponent, use all parts of both feet to propel the ball down the field.

- Push, nudge, and caress the ball enough to keep it close while kicking it hard enough to advance.
- Look ahead and to the sides to find clear paths to maneuver through. Focus on the opponent's waist to watch oncoming players and to keep the ball in your lower peripheral vision.
- Run on your toes so that you can stop quickly and change directions instantly.
- When pressured, use short steps so that you can keep control of the ball with frequent contact. When not pressured, take long strides and push the ball ahead, running after it.

Here's what to avoid:

- Dribbling into a pack. In close quarters, anyone can get possession of the ball—even the other team.
- Kicking the ball too far ahead. Anyone fast enough to intercept will be able to take possession before you catch up to the ball for your next kick.
- Running with your head down, staring at the ball. You'll lose sight of the rest of the game.

Everyone needs to develop a dribbling style. The best way to learn is to practice. When practicing by yourself gets boring, invite a few friends over with their soccer balls and try these games.

L.A. Freeway at Rush Hour
- Establish a playing field about fifteen by fifteen yards.
- Select someone to be the "traffic cop."
- Have everyone but the traffic cop dribble inside the field using all parts of their feet, moving the ball wherever they choose.
- When the traffic cop calls out, "Red light!" everyone must stop quickly and maintain control of their ball. When the traffic cop calls, "Green light!" everyone can move again.

Dribbling Tag
- Using the same fifteen-by-fifteen-yard field, select someone to be "It."
- "It" must tag each player.
- A player is out of the game when she's tagged or when her ball is kicked out of the playing field.
- The last player to be tagged becomes "It" for the next game.

AYSO Soccer Definitions

Attacker: The player in control of the ball, attempting to score a goal. Attackers need speed, power, good ball control, and accurate aim. Sometimes referred to as forward.

AYSO: American Youth Soccer Organization, a nationwide organization guided by five principles:
1. Everyone plays
2. Balanced teams
3. Open registration
4. Positive coaching
5. Good sportsmanship

Cleats: Projections on the soles of soccer shoes that provide support and a good grip on the soccer field.

Defender: The player whose primary duty is to prevent the opposing team from getting a good shot at the goal. Defenders need sufficient speed to cover opposing players, good tackling skills, and determination to win control of the ball.

Dribbling: Moving the ball along the ground by a series of short taps with one or both feet.

Goal: Scored when the entire ball crosses the line between the goalposts and underneath the crossbar. One goal equals one point.

Goalkeeper: The last line of defense. The goalkeeper is the only player who can use her hands during play within the penalty area.

Halfway line: A line that marks the middle of the field.

Halftime: A five- to ten-minute break in the middle of a game.

Midfielder: The player who supports the attack on the goal with accurate passes and hustles to get back to help the defense. Positioned in the middle of the field, she must have stamina for continuous running.

Open: A player who is not being marked or covered by a member of the opposing team is open.

Passing: Kicking the ball to a teammate.

Referee: An official who ensures the safety of all the players by enforcing the rules during a game.

Save: The prevention of an attempted goal, usually by the goalkeeper.

Scrimmage: A practice game.

Short-sided: A short-sided game is played with fewer than eleven players per team.

Substitution break: A quick break during which the coaches can put in new players and the players can grab a sip of water. Substitution breaks come a quarter and three quarters of the way through a game.

Throw-in: When the ball crosses the touchline, it is thrown back onto the field by a member of the team that did not touch the ball last. The thrower must keep both feet on or behind the touchline and throw the ball over her head.

Touchlines: Out-of-bounds lines that run along the long edges of the field.

Trapping: Gaining control of the ball using feet, thighs, or chest.

YOUR WORST nightmare is About to come true...

AGAIN...

AND AGAIN...

AND AGAIN...

Introducing Choose Your Own Nightmare, the interactive Multipath™ Movie where you control your fate.

From the spine-tingling Bantam Doubleday Dell book series, Choose Your Own Nightmare, come two eerie, animated, 3D creature features for your PC. The Halloween Party, where "scared to death" takes on new meaning thanks to a sorceress with murder on her mind. And Night of the Werewolf, a bloodcurdling thriller that reveals the animal within us all. As the monstrous thrills and chills unfold, use your keyboard to control the plot twists. With dozens of plot paths and multiple endings, play each movie again and again until all your worst nightmares come true.

Ask for this and other Multipath Movies at your local computer retailer and check out our website at WWW.BDE3D.COM

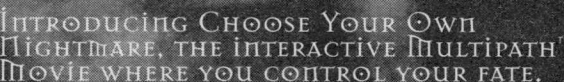

BRILLIANT™ DIGITAL *Entertainment*

MULTIPATH™ MOVIES
YOU DON'T JUST WATCH THEM, YOU CONTROL THE

For sales and customer service please call 1-800-227-9965